The LIGHT WITCH

for the friends and rellos in Oz:
Emma, Danielle, Happy, Spike, Alex, Jack, Vanessa,
Antonia, Michael, Tonia, Ian, Amy and Tom.

2nd Witch: By the pricking of my thumbs
Something wicked this way comes

William Shakespeare
Macbeth Act IV Scene 1

ORCHARD BOOKS
96 Leonard Street, London EC2A 4XD
Orchard Books Australia
32/45-51 Huntley Street, Alexandria, NSW 2015
ISBN 1 84362 187 8
First published in Great Britain in 2003
A paperback original
Text © Andrew Matthews 2003
The right of Andrew Matthews to be identified as the author
of this work has been asserted by him in accordance with
the Copyright, Designs and Patents Act, 1988.
A CIP catalogue record for this book is available from the British Library.
1 3 5 7 9 10 8 6 4 2
Printed in Great Britain

The LIGHT WITCH

Book 1:
Shadowmaster

Andrew Matthews

ORCHARD BOOKS

Other titles in *The Light Witch* Trilogy:

The Darkening
The Time of the Stars

Prologue: The Circle

The stone circle on the hill was old, far older than the town that lay westwards of it, and the road that flanked it to the east. Roman legions had marched by the circle, and Norman knights on war horses. Waves of bombers, and sleek airliners had droned over it. Invasions, wars, plagues and famines had been and gone, and left it unchanged.

Now, in the last light of a summer sunset, the circle had its own peculiar atmosphere, a restlessness that seethed and shifted in the gathering gloom. The red sunset's glare and lilac shadows showed every detail of the stones, every ridge and runkle, every pockmark and crack, forming faces, limbs, bodies frozen in a twisted dance.

A fox slunk from cover and began to cross the field where the circle stood, its coat dark crimson in the fading light. Ten metres away from the stone, the fox abruptly stopped and lowered its head. It sniffed, growled uneasily, put out a tentative paw and withdrew it swiftly, yelping. Its hackles rose in a spiky crest that ran the entire length of its back. The fox gave an angry bark and twisted away, skirting the circle and disappearing into a clump of long grass with a final flick of its brush.

For a time all was still and silent, and then a car came up the hill, travelling away from the town. The car parked at the side of the road. Its sidelights died. A door opened, the driver stepped out, walked solemnly into the centre of the circle and faced the tallest of the stones. The planet Mercury hovered in the sky above, its cold white spark quivering, as though it were underwater.

The stone spoke in a low voice that only the driver could hear.

'It has begun. She is coming. I can feel her. She is stronger than I estimated, but we both know that now and she does not. Until she realises her strength, you will have an advantage. Use it wisely. Serve me well, and all that you have wished for will be given to you.'

'All of it, my lord?' the driver asked.

'All,' replied the stone. 'You have laboured long,

with little reward to show for it. But now my power is growing. Soon I will grant you what you deserve. Go, and make yourself ready. Do not fail me.'

'I will not fail, my lord,' the driver said.

1

Moving Day

The Nesbits moved house in August. Dad chose the date, saying that he'd checked the omens and they were all good – or 'propitious' as he put it. Dido wasn't so sure, she'd done a little checking of her own, but when Mum didn't object, Dido didn't either. Dad had been really supportive about moving because of Mum's new job, and it seemed only fair to let him have his own way about something.

This turned out to be a mistake. Moving day was the hottest day so far that summer, the motorway was nose-to-tail traffic and Cosmo demonstrated her opinion of the cat-carrying basket by peeing inside it. Dad had to roll down the front windows to keep the smell from making his eyes water.

Dido, in the back seat next to Cosmo, caught the worst of the heady whiff rising from the basket. She managed to distract herself by making a Corn

Mother, weaving hay stalks between the arms of a cross formed by two hazel twigs tied together with garden twine. It took up so much of her concentration that she didn't register what was happening until Dad turned off the motorway, pulled into a lay-by and let Mum take over the driving.

Uh oh! thought Dido, knowing that it would lead to trouble. Her father was clever at a lot of things, but map-reading wasn't one of them.

Trouble came three kilometres later.

'Which exit do I take at this roundabout?' said Mum.

Dad peered at the road atlas, turned it around and peered again.

'Straight over.'

'Left,' said Dido.

Dad looked over his shoulder at her. 'What?'

'We should go left at the roundabout.'

'How d'you know? I'm the one with the map.'

'Dad, there was this road sign with Stanstowe marked on the left-hand turn.'

Dad blew air out through his teeth. 'This book is useless! The bits we need are right in the join between two pages. I ask you, what kind of idiot publishes a road atlas where—'

'Pete,' Mum interrupted gently, 'let Dido navigate. You must be tired.'

'I'm perfectly capable of navigating, thank you. I've been down this road before. I recognise that pub.'

The pub was at a T-junction. Mum stopped the car at a halt sign.

'Left or right?' she said.

'Left,' said Dad. 'I'm positive that it's left.'

Mum turned left.

'Er...wait a sec!' said Dad. 'Maybe we should have gone right.'

The road ran through woodland and fields of cows, broadened into a dual carriageway and then shrank into a winding lane.

Dido said, 'We're moving to the *countryside?*'

'No,' said Dad. 'Stanstowe is quite sizeable. It used to be a market town. I'm told that it's the most average place in Britain.'

'Does it have a cinema?'

'I think so.'

'A multiplex,' said Mum. 'It also has electricity, running water and a McDonalds. What else could an eleven-year-old girl need?'

'Sensible parents?' Dido suggested.

Mum grinned. 'Sorry, kiddo. You're stuck with us,

so you'd better get used to it.'

But Dido knew that she'd never get used to it; she'd spent her whole life trying.

The car began a climb up a steep hill. An avenue of trees cast a cool gloom over the road. Dido sensed something that made her frown, and the frown deepened as the car climbed. Then they came out of the trees, crested the brow of the hill and Dido saw what had been bothering her.

Behind a wire fence to her right stood a stone circle. Some of the stones were squat and roundish, others were tall and slender, shaped like the blades of cut-throat razors.

Dido felt a blast of ancient cold and shivered. 'You never told me about that!'

'You could have worked it out for yourself,' said Dad. 'The circle gave Stanstowe its name. In Old English *stane* means stone and *stowe* means a holy place. I wanted it to be a surprise for you.'

'It is, but not a nice one. It's creeping me out!'

Mum put on her teacher's voice. 'You should respect prehistoric sites, Dido. They're a part of our heritage.'

Cosmo suddenly let out a plaintive wail.

'You're right,' said Dido.

Mum thought that Dido was talking to her, but Dido was talking to the cat.

At the foot of the hill, Stanstowe spread out like a stain on a tablecloth. Dido saw row after row of identical houses, and two gigantic gasholders, rusted to the colours of a winter sunset.

'There we are,' said Dad. 'What d'you think, Dido?'

'All right, I suppose.'

But the stone circle had made her feel so uneasy that what she really wanted to say was, 'Turn around right now and get us out of here!'

The house was in the middle of a modern estate. The property developers had given the streets names like Cherry Tree Drive and Millstream Crescent, so that the residents could make-believe that they were living in a quaint little village.

Mum turned the car into Mistletoe Lane.

'Where's number seven, Pete?' she said. 'They all look the same to me.'

'Down here on the left,' said Dad. 'Or is it the right?'

Dido leaned forward and glanced through the windscreen. 'I think we should try the house with the removal van parked outside.'

The removal men were ferrying cardboard boxes from the lorry to the house. One of them paused when the car pulled up at the kerb.

'Afternoon!' he said. 'You got here then.'

No, thought Dido, we're stuck in a traffic jam outside Nottingham.

Dad got out of the car and fell into conversation with the removal men.

Mum said, 'While they do boys' talk, shall we unload the boot?'

Cosmo yowled.

'Hold on!' said Dido. 'We'll let you out later. You wouldn't like it with all those guys banging around. Just be patient, OK?'

Cosmo made a noise that was Cat for, 'OK!'

The boot was stuffed with boxes, carrier bags, books, and herbs growing in pots. The man talking to Dad saw Mum wrestling with a box and stepped forwards, saying, 'Here, let me take that.'

'It's fine, honestly,' said Mum.

'No, I insist. It's what you're paying me for, isn't it?'

The man put his hands on the box – and froze.

Mum stared straight into his eyes.

'Let go,' she said.

The man's hands flopped to his sides.

'Now go and find something else to do.'

The man turned and walked stiffly towards the house. When he reached the driveway he twitched and shook his head, as if he'd just woken up from a nap.

'Did you put a spell on him?' Dido said to Mum.

Mum winked, and clicked her tongue. 'You betcha!'

By the time the removal men left, it was twilight. The only room in the house that wasn't stacked with boxes was the kitchen, so Mum, Dad and Dido huddled there, watching Cosmo investigate the back garden. Dido noticed a thick bank of black cloud building up in the sky.

'We should clear the bedrooms next,' said Dad, trying to sound as though he meant it.

'Not until we've had something to eat – I'm starving!' said Mum. 'Why don't you and Dido look for a takeaway while I make a start upstairs? We can all get stuck in after we've eaten.'

'Sound plan! Indian, Chinese, pizza?'

'Anything.'

'Fish and chips?'

'Let Dido choose. Hurry up! If I don't eat something soon I may have to open a tin of cat food!'

*

Dad drove around the estate for five minutes and wound up at the opposite end of Mistletoe Lane.

'Must have gone wrong somewhere,' he muttered.

'What – you?' said Dido.

'I can do without the sarcasm, thanks.'

'Sor-ry! I say we drive to the end of the road, go right and take the third left.'

'Why?'

'Because it's the way into town.'

'How d'you know that?'

'My thumbs are itching.'

'You and your famous thumbs!' Dad snorted.

'Yes, me and my famous thumbs. Have they ever been wrong before?'

Dad left the question unanswered, which was how he admitted that Dido was right when he didn't want to.

They found the Golden Blossom Takeaway in a parade of shops at the edge of the estate. The owners obviously believed in keeping the public happy, because they sold Chinese food, fish and chips *and* curries. Dad and Dido were the only customers, but they still had to wait ages for their order. Dad sat down on the broad sill of the front window and stared at the floor. Dido watched a little boy goggling at a TV that was mounted on a bracket above the counter. He sang along with every advertising jingle.

'Must remember to do some charming before we go to bed,' said Dad, thinking aloud.

'What does that involve?'

'Not a lot. We walk anti-clockwise around the house seven times, waving rowan rods.'

'Oh.'

'Naked.'

Dido's eyes widened. 'Naked? You mean as in, "no clothes"?'

'Hmm.'

'What if the neighbours see us?'

'They'll call the police and we'll get arrested for indecent exposure.'

'*What?*'

'Calm down. No one's going to see us and if they do, your mother will cast a glamour on them.'

'What's one of those?'

'It makes people see things that aren't there, or not see things that *are* there.'

Hoping to catch Dad unawares, Dido said casually, 'How d'you do that then?'

Dad shook his head. 'Nice try, Dido, but I'm not

telling you until you're old enough to use it responsibly.'

A rumble of thunder shook the glass in the window.

'It's going to rain, Dad,' said Dido.

'Seems likely.'

'If it's raining when we do the charming, can we wear swimming costumes?'

'No. Rowan rods only work when you're naked.'

'Great!' said Dido, resisting a strong urge to tell Dad exactly what he could do with his rowan rods.

Dido and her parents were Light Witches and practised Light Magic. Light Magic and Shadow Magic had once worked in unison, two halves of the same whole known as Twilight Magic, but then something had split Twilight Magic into Light and Shadow, and now Light Witches were strictly forbidden to study Shadow Magic. Dido wasn't exactly clear why this was. As far as she was concerned magic was magic, and it was the way people used it that made it good or evil. It had occurred to her that perhaps Shadow Magic could somehow twist the people who used it, but when she asked Mum and Dad, they fobbed her off. Their standard reply to any of Dido's questions about Shadow Magic was, 'There'll be a time when it's right for you to know,' which was another way of saying *Shut up and wait until you're older*. Dido didn't see how she was expected to fully understand Light Magic without knowing something about its opposite, and had secretly started a research project.

General information about Shadow Magic was surprisingly easy to come by – in books and TV programmes, on the Internet, there were even hints and clues to be found in fairy stories, if you knew what you were looking for. Specific information – like what Shadow Witches believed in, what kinds of spells they cast and how they cast them – was more difficult to find, and Dido had only been able to unearth a few basic facts.

All Shadow Witches, whether male or female, were known as Shadowmasters. Light Witches made magic in groups or families, their powers usually being passed on from generation to generation. Shadowmasters were different. They worked alone, seldom mixing with their own kind, and the source of their power was mysterious. Shadow Magic seemed to take possession of them, sometimes after tempting them to use it and sometimes with no warning at all.

Some of the stuff that Dido had tried to get through over the past couple of years had been so badly written that it was unreadable, and some of it had been downright loopy. Dido had a theory about that; she thought that Shadowmasters deliberately muddled the truth about themselves, so that no one else would take it seriously, but Dido took it dead seriously. At times it was tricky to keep what she'd learned from her parents, but if they ever rumbled what she was up to, Dido would be in deep trouble.

2

A Dark Magnet

The first thing Dido noticed when she woke up was that her feet were hotter than the rest of her. She opened her eyes and saw Cosmo curled up at the end of the bed, her fur blue-black in the shaft of light streaming in through a gap in the curtains. Dido always left her bedroom door open for Cosmo, but even if she hadn't Cosmo would have got in. Closed doors presented no problems to the Nesbit cat – not even fridge doors.

Dido shifted to get her legs more comfortable, and as she did so she heard a scratchy, scrabbling sound coming from the cardboard boxes in the corner. Cosmo heard it too; her right ear swivelled round to track it and she began to purr.

'Cosmo,' said Dido, 'did you bring a mouse in here last night?'

Cosmo purred so loudly that the bed vibrated.

Dido sighed. Even though Cosmo was quite old, like all cats, she hunted birds and mice, but she didn't kill them; she brought them into the house to show off. She'd once caught a neighbour's pet rabbit which was almost as big as she was, and managed to haul it in through the cat flap. The neighbour hadn't been pleased. His four-year-old daughter had seen Cosmo run off with the rabbit, and he claimed that she'd been traumatised.

Dido cleared her mind, in preparation for what her parents called 'inseeing'. Her senses grew more and more intense until she could feel the touch of the light on her skin, and smell the specks of dust turning in the air; all the objects around her gave off a glow; Cosmo was surrounded by a pink haze of contentment, but another animal in the room was suffering from a stress that showed dark grey, like thick fog. It was a mouse all right, and it was petrified. It didn't understand where it was or what was going on. It had hidden among the boxes because that was the darkest place in the room.

Dido slipped out of bed and knelt on the floor, still inseeing. She started to hum a tune that Mum had taught her, keeping her voice low and soothing. The song was nameless, very old and no one had ever written it down.

The mouse liked it. It came around the side of the boxes and looked at Dido, its nose dabbing the air to test her scent. Dido didn't move, but carried on humming as though she didn't know that the mouse was there, and blocked out its awareness of Cosmo lying on the bed. The mouse decided that Dido was harmless and scurried a few centimetres closer. It didn't run away when Dido reached out for it; in fact, it ran on to her hand and let her pop it into the top pocket of her pyjamas.

Dido blinked and rubbed her eyes. Coming back from inseeing was like coming out of a cinema after watching an exciting movie – it took a few seconds to adjust to how ordinary the real world was.

Mum and Dad were already up, having breakfast in the kitchen. They'd found the boxes of pots, pans and crockery. The kitchen looked more like home with familiar things in it.

'Sleep all right?' Dad asked Dido.

'I must have. I can't remember anything about it.'

'Cornflakes or muesli?'

'Toast, please.'

Dad pulled a face and said, 'Slight problem with toast, I'm afraid.'

'No bread?'

'Plenty of bread, but we can't find the toaster.'

Dido smiled sweetly.

'See that cooker over there, Father dear?' she said. 'The people who made it put in this little gizmo they call a grill. What you do is, you turn on the grill, and—'

'OK, OK! This old wrinkly has lost the plot. Don't rub it in.'

'We'll get back to normal when we unpack the box with our brains in,' Mum promised. 'Tea or coffee?'

'Hot chocolate, please.' Dido touched her pocket. 'I have to go outside a second. Rescue mission.'

'What?' said Dad.

'Cosmo brought me a mouse.'

'Already? It didn't take her long to settle in. That cat is so laid-back. I sometimes wish I could be more like her.'

'We'd have to get a bigger cat flap, Dad.'

Dido released the mouse into the shrubbery at the edge of the back lawn. It turned its head this way and that, unsure of what to do, because the spell Dido had cast over it was still working.

'Hey, go find a mate and have lots of micettes!' Dido said.

The mouse darted off so quickly that it seemed to be there and gone at the same time.

The morning was boxes, boxes and more boxes. The lounge gradually took shape: Dad put up some bookshelves and assembled the stereo; the old red sofa fitted snugly into the bay of the front window. Dad carried in the TV, plonked it down on its black trolley and frowned.

'Why did we bring this thing?' he said. 'We hardly ever watch it.'

'I watch it,' said Dido. 'I have to, or I won't know what the other kids at school are talking about. I don't want to get labelled as a freak on my first day – it's going to be bad enough as it is.'

'You'll be all right. You'll soon make friends.'

'That's what you said when I went into the Juniors.'

'And I was right! You had lots of friends there.'

'Er, excuse me?' said Dido. 'There were people I hung out with, but they weren't exactly friends. Not the kind you can share stuff with.'

'What stuff?' said Dad.

'Who I really am.'

'Oh, *that* stuff.'

'Why does it have to be such a big secret anyway?'

Dad stopped what he was doing, which was tricky because he was halfway up a stepladder, his arms filled with books.

'People find it hard to overcome their prejudices,' he said. 'They've been brought up to fear people like us.'

'But if we explained—'

'They wouldn't listen. Frightened people are blind, deaf and don't behave rationally.'

'What, like they'd burn us at the stake or something?'

Dad's mouth set in a grim line. 'Dido, there are some things you don't tell jokes about, OK?'

Dido frowned. Despite what Dad thought, she knew that she was right – she'd never found it easy to make friends. Her secret somehow put a barrier between herself and people outside her family, no matter how hard she tried to overcome it. None of the other pupils at her previous school had succeeded in penetrating the barrier, and Dido had gained a reputation for being a bit of a loner.

*

Lunch was cheese sandwiches and tinned soup, then it was back to the boxes. By four o' clock, all the downstairs rooms were done and Dad called a halt.

'That's it – enough! I'm going box crazy,' he announced. 'My head's turning square.'

'You know,' said Mum, 'I've got the feeling that there used to be more to life than unpacking, but it's been so long that I've forgotten what it is.'

'Let's go out for a stomp, get some sunshine and fresh air.'

'Where?' Dido asked, and instantly knew what Dad would say.

'I thought we'd drive up to the circle and take a look round.'

'Round is the only way you *can* look at a circle, isn't it?' said Mum.

Cold sweat broke out on Dido's forehead. 'Can't we go somewhere else? That place seriously spooks me.'

'Which is why we should go there,' said Dad. 'I want to show you that there's nothing to be scared of.'

Dido remembered when Dad had taught her to ride a bicycle. He'd jogged alongside her, one hand holding the saddle, panting, 'There's nothing to be scared of. You won't fall over. You won't fall over!' Then he'd let go of the saddle and Dido had fallen over.

'Let's go some other time, Dad.'

'No time like the present. We'll grab a quick wash and skedaddle.'

'Skedaddle?'

'Nineteenth-century American slang term,' Mum said, 'meaning to run away or depart in haste. From the Greek *skedannumi*.'

'Save it for the classroom, Mum,' Dido said under her breath.

At the top of the hill, Dad parked the car on a grass verge. Dido got out reluctantly, keeping her eyes on the town below, not wanting to look at the circle. She could hear a lorry labouring up the hill; otherwise it was silent.

What happened to buzzing bees and twittering birds? she thought.

Dad came to stand beside her.

'Face it, Dido,' he said softly. 'Any fear looks pathetic if you stare at it hard enough.'

Dido turned. The stones were menacing. Their long shadows stretched out like dark fingers clutching at her. The stones seemed to dance in the shimmering heat, rippling with power. Dido had never felt anything like it before, yet she almost recognised it.

This is like trying to name an actor in a movie, she thought. Like you *know* you know the name, but you can't remember what it is.

'Come on,' said Dad. 'This is supposed to be a walk, not a stand.'

Up close, the circle was far less imposing. Time had caught up with it. The wire fence was trampled down in places and the ground was littered with crumpled lager cans, cellophane wrappers and cigarette ends. The stones had been defaced with spray-can graffiti –

DIBBO + KAYLEIGH; MUFC; BIVCO + LOOMES –

plus the usual swearwords and swastikas.

'Why do people do that?' said Dido.

'To let us know they're there,' said Dad. 'It's been going on for a long time. Look!' He pointed to marks that had been deeply engraved in one of the stones – ELD 1864. 'That's where vandalism turns into history.'

Mum looked sad and annoyed. 'Why can't they just leave the place alone?'

Because it doesn't want them to, thought Dido. It uses the graffiti as camouflage, so it looks harmless, when it isn't.

'It seems a popular place,' said Dad. 'I'd guess that local youths gather here at night to imbibe alcoholic liquor and dally with their consorts.'

'Huh?' said Dido.

Mum provided a translation. 'Teenagers come here to get drunk and make out.'

But why the circle? thought Dido. There have to be quiet places in Stanstowe that are easier to get to. It must draw them like a dark magnet.

Dad said, 'Appropriate, when you come to think of it. These stones are fertility symbols. The short ones are female, the tall ones are male.'

'How come?' said Dido.

Dad's face went pink. 'Well...um, you know.' He waved his hands in the general direction of his trousers. 'They're shaped like people's bits.'

'Got it!' Dido said quickly, before Dad went into more detail than she needed. 'Why was it built up here?'

'Because it's closer to the sky,' said Mum.

Inside the circle were the remains of a bonfire, a black scar on the yellow grass. Something leapt up at

Dido: she caught a quick burst of chanting; pale limbs flashing in flickering firelight and...

'Can you feel it?' said Mum.

'What?'

'Like that feeling you get in old churches.'

'No.'

'What feeling does it give you?'

'Hunger,' said Dido. 'Didn't you say yesterday that there was a McDonalds in town?'

She was lying; she wasn't hungry, she just wanted to get away from the circle before something happened.

Dido had no idea of what the something might be, and no desire to find out.

3
The Pentacle

Two days later, the last of the delivery firm's boxes were empty, and the Nesbits were well and truly moved in. Dad had the spare bedroom as his office. After he'd installed his computer and piled the bookshelves with technical manuals, it looked just like the office in the old house. Most of the manuals had Dad's name on, because writing manuals was one of the ways he earned a living. He also wrote monthly columns in two computer magazines – he was Ed Behr in one and Rick Joad in the other – as well as book reviews, articles and anything else he was asked to write. Dad's official title was 'freelance science journalist' but he always called himself a 'hack'.

While Dad was busy sending e-mails, Dido and Mum turned the summer house into a sanctuary, a place for meditation and magic. The summer house was in the back garden, screened from prying eyes by a mock-orange tree and a beech hedge. Mum put the statue of the Goddess in the middle of a high shelf. The statue wasn't actually a statue, just a large limestone pebble, but if you looked at it from the right angle and used your imagination, you could make out the shape of a woman lying on her side, her head resting on the palm of her left hand.

Mum squinted at the Goddess, shifted her a centimetre and said, 'D'you think she'll like Stanstowe, Dido?'

'She'll soon let us know if she doesn't.'

'How about you – are you going to like it here?'

'I'll get used to it.'

'Is that a yes or a no?'

'It's a let's-wait-and-see.'

'Worried about the new school?'

Dido shrugged.

'I am,' said Mum. 'I'm petrified. I keep looking at myself in the mirror and saying, "*I am a Deputy Head*", but it won't sink in.'

'What does a Deputy Head do, exactly?'

'It depends, but they usually do the jobs that the Head doesn't like.'

'Will you have to take assemblies, and say prayers and stuff?'

Mum flinched, as if she'd been hoping that Dido wouldn't ask.

'Yes,' she said.

Dido nodded at the Goddess. 'What will she make of that?'

'She'll understand.'

'You always say that. You make it sound like she understands everything.'

'She does,' said Mum. 'Otherwise she wouldn't be a goddess, would she?'

By the time all the jars of herbs, dried roots and oils were in place, the sanctuary looked and smelled right. Mum prayed silently – not with hands together and eyes closed, simply staring at the Goddess and thinking.

Dido joined in. She wasn't sure what she should pray for, so she left it vague.

'If you can help things work out around here, it would be nice if you did, OK?'

At two o' clock, Mum and Dido drove into Stanstowe. Mum managed to find her way through the labyrinthine one-way system and they left the car in a multi-storey car park.

As she walked along, Dido clocked a few

landmarks for future reference: the public park with a Victorian war memorial topped by a huge stone lion; the blue-and-red brick Town Hall that looked like a Gothic wedding cake; the bookshop that had once been a Baptist church. Stanstowe had more than its fair share of pubs, which might have had something to do with the atmosphere. The town wasn't just busy, it was frenetic – people rushing around with their right arms raised to their faces, talking into mobile phones; groups of sullen-faced teenagers elbowing people aside; mothers barging pushchairs through the crowds, like ram-raiders.

Not so much hustle and bustle as hassle and bash, Dido thought.

The main objective of the expedition into the town centre was to join the public library. When they finally located the library – next door to a coffee bar called BEENZ – Mum and Dido staggered into the peaceful foyer, sighing with relief.

'Busy sort of place, isn't it?' Mum said.

'Not in here it isn't,' said Dido. 'I think we're the only customers. Doesn't anybody read in Stanstowe?'

'Don't exaggerate, Dido.'

But Dido wasn't exaggerating. Apart from the staff and an elderly man dozing behind a newspaper, the library was deserted.

While Mum filled in forms and gave the librarians proof that she and her family really existed, Dido went exploring. She was hoping to dig up some information on the stone circle that might explain why she'd reacted so strongly to it. The local history section of the reference library seemed a likely starting point.

If Stanstowe was proud of its history, there wasn't much written evidence of it – just a handful of books with such promising titles as, *Stanstowe in the Swingin' Sixties* and *The Silk Weaving Industry in Stanstowe: A Pictorial Guide*. Then Dido noticed that several books were sticking out from the shelf, as though something were pushing them forward. When she hunkered down for a closer look, Dido saw the edge of a brown leather cover. A book had somehow got jammed behind the others. She reached out to prise it loose, and felt – or thought that she felt – the book wriggle away.

'Not so fast!' Dido whispered. 'You don't escape my clutches that easily.'

She removed several volumes from the shelf, lifted

out the hidden book and examined it. The gold lettering on the spine was so ornamental that it took Dido a while to figure out the title: *Transactions of the Stanstowe Antiquarian and Folklore Society: 1889–1890.*

Dido carried the book to the nearest table. She suspected that she was the first person to consult it in a long time, because it opened with a loud crack and a puff of dust. The edges of the pages were brittle and ginger, but the rest of the paper was creamy white and the print still looked fresh.

Dido's luck held. The title of the first article was: '*The Speaking Stones: An account of the folklore traditions concerning the stone circle on Stanstowe Hill*', by *The Right Honourable Sir Edwin Langley-Davis, PhD, MA, BA (Hons), Member of Parliament for Stanstowe.*

Bingo! thought Dido, and settled down to read.

Sir Edwin Langley-Davis couldn't have won any awards for his prose-style. The article started with a description of the archaeological history of the site. Fortunately this was brief, because as it turned out no one had ever done a proper excavation of the circle, and it wasn't long before Dido got to the juicy stuff.

The circle's most common nomenclature, 'The

Speaking Stones', may derive from the Old English 'speke' meaning 'brushwood', perhaps a reference to the copious woods that flourished on Stanstowe Hill in prehistoric times, but it may also be a corruption of the name of some long-forgotten minor deity or *spiritus loci*. A medieval document in my possession refers to the circle as 'The Spielor Stones', but the etymology of this term has stubbornly resisted all my attempts to unravel it.

As is common with sites of such antiquity, many folk tales surround the circle. Cornelius Hooper, Stanstowe's inestimable seventeenth-century collector of rumour and gossip, relates a story of how a party of drunken revellers, caught dancing and carousing at an hour when they should have been at prayer, were cursed by the Abbot of Stanstowe Priory and turned to stone. Another tale holds Merlin responsible for the circle, and claims that he used his magic arts to transport the stones through the air from Ireland. There are also the usual sorts of stories about Druid priests using the circle as a setting for the performance of human sacrifices, but these, if they were performed at all, are more likely to have taken place in sacred forest groves.

That the circle has exercised considerable influence over the imagination of Stanstowians may be surmised from the number of superstitions attached to it. Cornelius

Hooper records that an old woman told him that if a person stands in the centre of the circle at noon on Midsummer's Day and spits seven times to the east and seven times to the west, the Devil will appear and grant his heart's desire. The same indomitable old dame related that, at midnight on Christmas Eve the stones of the circle return to human form and bow down in adoration of the Infant Saviour. Anorther sorpastution moontimes hatt....

Huh? thought Dido.

She read through the last sentence again.

Aniver sappertation monsoons hut...

The sentence and the rest of the page were complete gobbledygook. Each time Dido tried to read on, the letters shifted around and turned the words into nonsense. Someone must have cast a scrambling spell on the book.

The back of Dido's neck prickled. Gingerly, she half closed her eyes and used her power of inseeing.

The spell was old and cantankerous, shaped like a grey spider-thing that clutched jealously at the pages with its long hairy legs. Dido had never come across anything like it and wasn't sure what to do. The spell's eyes were tiny beads of malice, and it didn't seem to take kindly to being inseen. It moved its mouth parts and exuded a thin thread of drool.

'Eew, gross!' Dido muttered. 'No need to get your knicks in a knot, I get the message – butt out, yeah?'

She released the spell from her inseeing and it sank back into the page. Dido left the book where it was, not wanting to touch it now that she knew what it contained, and went to find Mum.

Mum was at the main desk. She was the proud possessor of two library cards – one for her and one for Dido – but what she'd had to go through to get them had set her fuming.

'The librarians in this place are so dozy they're practically comatose,' she told Dido. 'The woman who entered our names on the database could only type with one finger! It would have been quicker to use a quill and a roll of parchment. Let's get out of here before I do something drastic, like making all their computers—'

'Y-e-e-s?' said Dido.

'I'm not saying. It might give you ideas.'

Outside in the street, Mum calmed down enough for Dido to ask, 'Mum, why would anyone put a scrambling spell on an old book?'

'They wouldn't,' said Mum. 'Witches used scrambling spells to protect their grimoires, but that was centuries ago.'

'Grim what?' said Dido, tactfully playing dumb.

'Books of magic. Nowadays we use locking spells – far more effective. Scrambling spells are only used to play tricks on people.'

'Like a practical joke?'

'Yes.'

Dido's mind started to turn things over. So what's the big deal with the article on the stone circle? she thought. Who had it in for the Right Honourable Sir Edwin Langley-Davis?

A sudden memory flash took her back to the circle and she remembered the carving on one of the stones – ELD 1864. ELD – Edwin Langley-Davis.

'I wonder,' Dido murmured to herself. 'Hey, Mum, d'you reckon that—?'

But Mum wasn't there. Mum was two metres behind, rooted to the pavement, staring straight ahead, her mouth open in amazement.

Dido followed the direction of her gaze.

Fixed to the side of one of the buildings straight ahead was a large sign.

POP INTO THE PENTACLE
STANSTOWE'S SHOPTASTIC
NEW MALL!

Below the letters was a picture of a five-pointed star enclosed in a circle: a pentagram, the symbol of Shadow Magic.

Dido walked back to Mum and touched her on the arm. Mum started as though she'd been bitten. 'You all right?' asked Dido.

'Yes,' said Mum, blinking rapidly. 'That sign just took me by surprise for a second.'

'Isn't that the symbol of—?'

'Yes.'

'It's a bit off, using it as a sign for a shopping mall, isn't it?'

'It doesn't mean anything,' said Mum, trying to sound nonchalant. 'It's only a coincidence.'

Dido wasn't so sure; in fact, she was beginning to get the uneasy sensation that Stanstowe was a much more unusual town than she'd first thought.

4
The School Cat

In the morning, the weather began unpromisingly and rapidly declined. There was a thunderstorm, with real rain that rebounded on itself as though it were trying to jump back into the sky. Cosmo leapt on to the back of the sofa in the lounge and gazed out of the front window, lashing her tail and purring whenever the lightning flickered. In *The Complete Book of Cat Care*, it said that cats were distressed by thunderstorms, but Cosmo obviously hadn't read that book.

As Dido was helping Mum to load the dishwasher after breakfast, Mum said, 'I've got a meeting with the Head this morning. Coming with me?'

'What for?'

'You could take a look around, get to know the place so next week won't be such a shock.'

Dido knew one of Mum's hidden orders when she

heard it. 'Yeah, good idea,' she said. 'It beats staying indoors, watching the rain.'

The storm grew worse. When Mum and Dido set off, the windscreen wipers could barely cope with the downpour and Mum had to drive at milk-float speed; even then, she nearly missed the sign pointing right: The Prince Arthur Comprehensive School.

'Who was Prince Arthur?' Dido asked.

'Henry the Eighth's older brother,' said Mum. 'He died before he could come to the throne.'

'Would he have been King Arthur the First or King Arthur the Second?'

'Interesting question.'

'How old was he when he died?'

'I'm not sure – fifteen, sixteen? Something like that.'

Dido thought about it. 'Isn't it a bit iffy to name a school after a dead teenager?' she said.

'It's something to do with the land the school was built on. I don't know the details. I'm only an English teacher, remember?'

'No you're not, you're a Deputy Head.'

'But I'll still be teaching English classes.'

The car passed through a gateway, on to a curving drive, and Dido had her first glimpse of the school lit by lightning, like the opening shot of a corny horror movie. The central building was old, with arched windows, sloping roofs, a clock tower and ivy growing up the walls. On either side were modern blocks, boxes made of glass and plastic. Dido couldn't make up her mind which part looked more out of place, the old or the new.

Mum and Dido made a quick, wet dash from the car to the main entrance. The inside of the school was a let-down. Dido had been hoping for wooden panelling and dusty chandeliers, but it looked like any other school: grey floor tiles, a reception area, a glass cabinet filled with sports trophies. One wall was lined with photographs of the staff, including one of Mum – Our new Deputy Head, Mrs Faye Nesbit BA, MEd.

A man was leaning against the reception desk, reading through a list attached to a clipboard. He had dark, curly hair streaked with grey, and a craggily handsome face that made Dido think that he must have been quite a hunk in his younger days. He was wearing a dark blue sweatshirt, faded denim jeans and scruffy trainers.

'PE teacher,' Dido guessed.

The man looked up, saw Mum and smiled broadly.

'Faye! How's the move going?'

'We're getting there thanks, Alan. This is my daughter Dido. Dido, this is Dr Parker, your Headmaster.'

Dr Parker reduced the size of his smile before he turned it on Dido. He had strikingly brown magnetic eyes that drew Dido in so that she was unable to look away. His natural air of authority made her guess that it didn't pay anyone to get on his wrong side.

'Ah yes!' said Dr Parker. 'You're going into Seven North, aren't you?'

'Yes, Sir,' Dido said.

'You'll have Mr Purdey as your form tutor. He's one of our most experienced teachers.' Dr Parker smiled. 'Dido,' he said. 'That's an unusual name.'

'It runs in the family,' Mum said smoothly, failing to add that in the sixteenth century, the original bearer of the name had been condemned for practising witchcraft, strapped into a ducking-stool and drowned. 'Is it all right if Dido does some exploring while we have our meeting?'

'Of course. I'll check with the site supervisor that the alarm system's been shut down.'

'Don't worry, Dr Parker!' Dido said. 'Alarms don't—' She'd been going to say that she could prevent alarms from going off, but changed her mind when she saw the frantic expression in Mum's eyes. 'I mean, I won't touch anything.'

'We'll be about an hour,' said Dr Parker. 'If we're any longer, you have my permission to come into my office and drag your mother out. Should you get lost—'

'Dido won't get lost,' said Mum. 'She has a strong homing instinct, don't you, Dido?'

Dido grinned and thought, Yeah, well, you *could* put it that way.

Now that Dido was alone, she used inseeing. The double doors in front of her led into the main hall – but that wasn't difficult to work out, because the stage was visible through the safety-glass panels. Where did the doors on her right lead to? Dido concentrated: a staircase ran up to the first floor, which was... Dido's ears sifted the air, listening for the echoes of voices.

'*Asseyez-vous, mes élèves, et ouvrez vos livres!*'

The Languages Department. Eager to find out if she was right, Dido pushed open the doors and climbed the stairs. Result! There was a poster of the Eiffel Tower, and a photographic display of kids on a cross-channel ferry, pulling faces at the camera.

And a cat.

The cat was seated at the far end of the corridor: a big, silver tabby with yellow eyes. Its tail was wrapped around its paws, and it seemed nowhere near as surprised to see Dido as she was to see it. The cat glared at her, as if she were trespassing on its territory, but at the same time Dido sensed something else.

She crouched slowly, extended her right arm and clicked her thumbnail against the nail of her forefinger.

'Hello, puss! Come on then.'

No reaction; the cat was playing hard to get.

Dido tried a friendly purr – zilch. She thought, Hey, what is this? I'm good with cats. They like me. This cat needs persuading that I'm irresistible.

Dido risked a charm. Humming a tune that was a variation of the one she'd used on the mouse, she circled her hands around each other, as if winding in a thread that would bring the silver tabby closer.

The cat flattened its ears against its skull and hissed, puffing up its fur until it looked twice its normal size, tail held up flagpole-straight.

Dido only had time to think, Huh? before the charm came back at her like an elastic band snapping, filling her nose with the sour-milk stink of decaying magic. As she recoiled from the smell, the cat shot past her with an angry yowl.

Dido's head pounded. That's not supposed to happen! she thought. Cats can't throw off an animal charm unless...

...Unless they had been protected by a stronger charm, like the one Mum had put on Cosmo.

The shadows in the corridor flowed together, forming nightmare shapes that worked on Dido's confusion, trying to turn it into fear. She fought the fear, pushing it down until the shadows returned to their proper places.

Dido thought quickly, searching for common-sense explanations, but there weren't any; which only left one conclusion.

'We are not alone,' Dido whispered.

Precisely an hour after Dr Parker had disappeared with Mum, the door of his office opened and they stepped into the corridor, where Dido was waiting.

'I hope that wasn't too boring for you, Dido,' Dr Parker said.

'No, sir. I met the school cat.'

'I'm sorry?' Dr Parker said with a frown.

'The school cat? A big silver tabby, not very friendly.'

'Oh, him! He's nothing to do with the school. He hangs around and scrounges food from the pupils at break.'

I bet he does! thought Dido. And if they don't hand any over, he grabs them by the throat and shakes it out of them.

'I've asked the pupils not to encourage him, but...' Dr Parker held up his hands in a what-can-you-do? gesture.

'Kids and cats, eh?' said Mum. 'We've got a cat, so I know how it is. Are you a cat person, Alan?'

Dido knew the answer, and it slipped out before she could stop it. 'Cats make Dr Parker sneeze, don't they, Sir?'

Dr Parker raised an eyebrow and looked sharply at Dido. 'Yes, as a matter of fact, they do. How on earth did you—?'

'Good guess!' said Dido.

Mum was irritated, but didn't let it show until she and Dido were in the car.

'Honestly, Dido! What were you playing at? You could have given yourself away, talking about the Head's cat allergy like that.'

'I wasn't playing at anything. There was this cat upstairs, and...'

Dido told Mum what had happened.

'Don't be so melodramatic, Dido!' Mum said. 'You must have made a mistake, that's all.'

'I didn't! The charm wouldn't take. It slipped off like – like something slipping off an extremely slippery thing. Dad said Stanstowe is the most average town in Britain, didn't he?'

'Yes, but what's that got to do with—?'

'So, how many witches are there in the average town?'

Mum wouldn't go down that road. 'Charming is tricky with larger animals like cats, Dido. You probably forgot something. It wouldn't be the first time, would it?'

Mum was using her teacher's voice again, which meant that she wasn't open to negotiation.

Dido thought, Here's where she tells me I'm young and inexperienced. After three – one, two, three!

'It's early days for you yet, Dido,' Mum said. 'You can't expect to run before you can walk. When you've had more experience, you'll be able to...'

Dido didn't listen to the rest: there was no point; she already knew it off by heart.

5
Voodini

On Monday morning Dido did her best to stay calm, but it wasn't easy with Mum flapping around like a loose sheet in a hurricane. When Dido came downstairs for breakfast, Mum eyed her white shirt and pleated navy blue skirt and frowned.

'Where's your school jumper?' Mum said.

'In my bag.'

'Why aren't you wearing it?'

'Mum, it's twenty degrees already. It's too hot to wear a jumper.'

Mum drew her lips into a tight circle. 'But you're the new Deputy Head's daughter,' she said. 'The staff will be expecting you to set a good example.'

Dido had known that this moment was bound to come, and steeled herself to say what had to be said.

'I'm not the new Deputy Head's daughter, Mum, I'm me. If I tried to be anyone else it would be dishonest. I don't tell you how to run the school, you don't tell me how to be a pupil, agreed?'

Mum's mouth slackened.

'You're right,' she said. 'I'm stressed. I shouldn't take it out on you. Am I being a cow?'

'No, but you're acting like you're about to have one.'

Dad breezed into the dining room, clocked Mum's outfit and wolf-whistled.

'I've never fancied a Deputy Head before,' he said. 'If I give you cheek, will you keep me behind after school and—?'

'Pete,' said Mum, 'not now, OK?' She looked at her watch. 'Come on, Dido.'

'I haven't had any breakfast yet,' said Dido.

'We'll get something on the way. I want to be at school early.'

'And I don't. I want to be there at the same time as the other kids. I'll catch a bus.'

'But—'

'Mum, if you drive me, everybody's going to know I'm your daughter. They're bound to find out sooner or later, but if it's later I'll have a chance to make some friends first. I'll need them when people start giving me a hard time because my mother's a Deputy Head.'

Mum sighed.

'Please yourself,' she said. 'I haven't got time to argue with you.' She kissed Dido on the cheek and Dad on the lips. 'See you both later.'

'Good luck,' said Dad.

'Yes, good luck, Mum,' Dido said.

Dad waited until Mum had closed the front door behind her, then turned to Dido and said, 'You were a bit rough on her, weren't you? She's got a lot on her plate.'

'Just telling it like it is.'

'Do you really think that people are going to give you a hard time?'

'Why wouldn't they?'

Dad looked puzzled. He had no idea, he'd never had a teacher as a parent.

There was another Year Seven pupil – a boy – waiting at the bus stop. He looked nervous, and he'd obviously had a haircut recently, because he kept on running his right hand over the back of his neck. When he spotted Dido, he left his place in the queue and joined her at the back. He was shorter than Dido. His clothes were too big for him and there was such a massive knot in his tie that the tie only came halfway down the front of his shirt. He had short black hair and brown eyes with long lashes.

'You too, eh?' he said.

'Me too what?' said Dido.

'You're on the way to Prince Arthur Comp. I noticed the uniform.'

'It's not a uniform. I always dress this way,' Dido said, a hint of a smile twitching at the corner of her lips.

The boy frowned, then laughed and said, 'Oh yeah, I get it! Very funny. What form are you going to be in?'

'Seven North.'

'Wow, cool! So am I.'

The boy reached out. Dido thought he was offering to shake hands, until she saw the plastic handcuffs dangling from his fingers. In a loud, dramatic voice, the boy said, 'Voodini is the name, and escapology is the game!'

'Esca-what?'

'Escapology. I escape from ropes and chains and stuff.' The boy shook the handcuffs. 'Tie me up with these.'

'Excuse me?'

'Tie me up.'

Dido was embarrassed: people in the bus queue were turning to stare. To keep the boy quiet she took the handcuffs, placed them on his wrists and pressed them shut.

The boy smiled and started to wiggle his arms.

'Handcuffs are child's play to Voodini!' he announced. 'In just a few seconds, I shall—'

He struggled and strained. His face went red and beads of sweat broke out on his forehead.

'Child's play,' he muttered. 'If I can just—'

Someone in the bus queue sniggered. It had gone beyond a joke. Dido held the boy still and pressed the release catch on the handcuffs.

'Thanks,' the boy said. 'I don't understand it. It worked perfectly when I practised last night.'

'You practise a lot?' said Dido.

'Two hours a day.'

'And you're that good?'

The boy didn't twig that Dido was joking.

'You have to be dedicated if you want to turn professional,' he said. 'What's your name?'

'Dido Nesbit. What's yours?'

The boy said, 'Scott,' and then something that Dido didn't catch.

'Sorry?' said Dido.

'Um, Scott Pink. And don't bother cracking any jokes about it, because I've heard them all before.'

'Oh?'

'Like looking at the world through rose-coloured glasses, being a colourful character and—'

'Actually, I wasn't going to make any jokes. I think it's a nice name.'

'You do?'

'Sure. It's kind of different. Original, you know?'

Scott's face lit up.

I shouldn't have said that, thought Dido. He's going to latch on to me and I won't be able to get rid of him.

'I'm working on a mind-reading act too,' said Scott. 'It pays to be versatile. Think of a—'

'Scott, here comes the bus,' said Dido. 'It's time to wake up and go to school.'

Year Seven were the only pupils in school that Monday morning. They were herded into the assembly hall to listen to a speech from Dr Parker. Mum and the other Deputy Head were on the stage. Mum had her Mrs Nesbit face on, eyes fixed straight ahead and a mouth that looked as though it never smiled.

The hall was noisy when Dr Parker walked in, but

when he looked around, silence followed the sweep of his eyes and he immediately had his audience's complete attention. He talked about realising potential and working as a team. He said that the school was a community in which everybody was responsible for everybody else. The few jokes he threw in didn't go down well, because the Year Sevens were too nervous to laugh.

Dido sneaked a glance at the teachers who were seated around the sides of the hall, to see if she could guess which one of them was Mr Purdey.

Dr Parker said, 'I'm going to dismiss you form by form. When I call out the name of your form, go into the playground, line up and wait for your form tutor. First, Seven North.'

Dido stood up. Scott, who was sitting next to her, stayed where he was, lost in Dr Parker's spell.

Dido nudged him with her foot.

'Shift your butt, Voodini!' she said.

'Huh?'

'The Head said Seven North. That's us.'

'Oh, right,' said Scott, sounding unenthusiastic.

Dido had known Scott for less than an hour, but she'd already noticed that when he wasn't being Voodini, he was vague and almost painfully shy. She wondered who the real Scott Pink was.

Mr Purdey turned out to be a tall slim man with thinning brown hair. He wore a beige corduroy jacket with black trousers, and a pair of steel-rimmed spectacles that framed his pale-blue eyes. He waited patiently for the form to gather round him, then said quietly, 'Pay attention, Seven North. I'm going to take you to your form base. Follow me in single file, please, and try not to straggle, or you might get lost.'

He led Seven North to the entrance doors of one of the modern buildings.

'Go to the top floor and line up in the corridor outside C17,' he said, 'but don't go into the room until I tell you to.'

Seven North obediently toiled up three flights of stairs and waited in the corridor. When Mr Purdey arrived he strolled along the line, making eye contact with each member of the form.

'C17 is your form base,' he said. 'It's part of the Design and Technology suite. Instead of desks, the room is equipped with extremely delicate and expensive drawing tables. If you fiddle with them, something might break and you'd have to take a large bill home for your parents to pay. You may go in and sit down, but don't touch anything.'

Once the form had settled into the room, Mr Purdey said, 'Since we're going to be together for a year, I'd better set a few ground rules. You're not allowed to eat or drink in the form base, and you're responsible for keeping it tidy. At morning and afternoon registration, wait outside the building until I arrive. If you have something you want to say to me during registration, please put up your hand – don't call out. Is that clear?'

There was a low murmur.

'Good,' said Mr Purdey. 'Now I'm going to take the register. Thomas Andrews?'

While Mr Purdey recited the names of her classmates, Dido gave them the once-over. It was difficult to tell anything about most of them, but one girl stood out. She was in a back corner of the room, on her own, but she didn't seem to mind. She had long fair hair tied in bunches, a pretty, blue-eyed face and a wide, Oscar-winner's smile.

'Philippa Trevelyan?' said Mr Purdey.

'Present, Mr Purdey!' the girl said brightly.

Dido wondered why Philippa Trevelyan was trying so hard, and as she was wondering, her thumbs began to itch.

6
The Terrible Trio

For the next hour and a half, Mr Purdey handed out timetables, homework logs, tutorial booklets and went through the uniform rules. He was brisk and efficient, but seemed neither friendly nor unfriendly, and Seven North weren't quite sure what to make of him. Some of the class weren't sure what to make of Dido and Scott either. In the rest of the classroom, girls sat with girls and boys sat with boys, and Dido noticed a lot of sideways glances directed at her and Scott, accompanied by behind-the-hand giggling. It was depressing. Dido's plan to start the term quietly and not draw attention to herself had already misfired. She had two choices: dump Scott and go ultra-girly, or stay with him and chance getting stick.

Scott was blissfully unaware of the glances and sniggers.

'Now copy your timetables into your homework

logs,' Mr Purdey declared. 'You can talk, but don't let it get too noisy.'

Dido finished copying her timetable in just a few minutes and looked over to see how Scott was getting on.

'Er, Scott?' she said.

'Mm?'

'You've put French in for Thursday, Lesson One.'

'So?'

'It's Maths. You've got Tuesday and Thursday mixed up.'

Scott checked, saw that Dido was right, groaned and started crossing out. His timetable was slowly transformed into a tangle of scribbles.

'I can't make sense of this!' he whined. 'And I don't get the carousel thing. Why is Drama sometimes Music and sometimes Design?'

'It's Drama this term, Music after Christmas and Design in the summer,' Dido explained. 'Why don't you stick the print-out into your homework log when you get home?'

'Because I'll have lost it by then. I'm always losing things.'

'Put it somewhere safe.'

'If I do, I'll forget where the safe place is.'

'I thought escape artists had to be incredibly organised.'

Scott shrugged.

'I'm organised when I do escapology,' he said. 'It's life I have problems with.'

Dido opened her pencil case, took out a Pritt stick and gave it to Scott. He twisted the base too far and the sticky stuff fell out of the tube on to the floor. In the scramble to pick it up, Scott banged his head on the edge of the table and the table shifted across the floor tiles with a screech that made everybody wince. Scott surfaced with a ketchup-coloured blush, tried to push the sticky stuff back into the tube and got most of it on his fingers.

'I'll do it for you!' Dido said with a sigh.

Scott had made her mind up for her: she couldn't dump him, he wouldn't survive on his own.

Break came at last. Dido filed out behind Scott, looking forward to sinking the carton of orange juice in her bag, but before she reached the door, Mr Purdey said, 'Dido Nesbit, I'd like to talk to you, please.'

'I'll see you outside,' Dido told Scott.

When he was sure that the last of Seven North was safely out of earshot, Mr Purdey said, 'I just wanted to let you know that I appreciate what a difficult position you're in.'

'Sir?'

'Because you're a Deputy Head's daughter. Some pupils may make unkind remarks about it.'

'I can handle it,' Dido said.

The determination in her voice made Mr Purdey raise his eyebrows.

'I'm sure you can,' he said. 'But I don't think you ought to take matters into your own hands. The school's got a strict policy on verbal bullying. If it happens to you, tell me straightaway and let me deal with it.' Mr Purdey sighed. 'I don't know about you, but I'm gasping for a cup of tea.'

'You can't have it here, sir,' said Dido. 'Drinking's not allowed in the form base.'

Mr Purdey laughed. 'You're quick on the uptake, aren't you? I'll have to watch what I say when I'm around you. Off you go, now.'

It was sweltering outside. Most of Seven North kept in the shadows of C block as they swigged from cans, and munched crisps and chocolate bars. A few compared notes with pupils from other forms. Scott was being Voodini for the benefit of three boys. They laughed, but Dido could hear that they were laughing *at* Scott, not with him. She was about to stride to the rescue, but caught a snatch of conversation that made her hesitate.

'I'm going to have my own laptop. It comes with a built-in modem, and a colour printer. It's quite expensive, but my mother says that it's important for my education. She's driving into London this afternoon to pick it up.'

Dido turned her head and saw Philippa Trevelyan talking to two other girls from Seven North, Mandy Dean and Charlotte Barnes. Mandy was holding a copy of *Glitz Girlz* magazine, which, as far as Dido was concerned, said a lot about her. *Glitz Girlz* was aimed at pre-teen girls who wanted to grow up in a hurry, full of features on cosmetics and chat-up advice. Dido found *Glitz Girlz* terminally depressing, because in her opinion there ought to be more to life than pulling boys. There was more to *her* life anyway.

What had attracted Dido's attention wasn't what Philippa was saying, but the way she was saying it. She wasn't talking so much as running off at the mouth, and she sounded overeager, as if she were desperate to make friends with somebody.

'I won't be able to use it until after my ballet class though,' Philippa said. 'It's a pain, but if I don't keep up my lessons, I might not pass the audition for stage school.'

Mandy and Charlotte seemed to be hanging on her every word, as though Philippa were living their dreams.

Except that Dido knew that she wasn't: Philippa was lying through her perfectly even teeth because she had something to hide. Dido's thumbs itched so badly that she had to scratch them with the nails of her index fingers.

Is this a premonition, a warning, or what? she thought.

The worst thing about having intuitive thumbs was waiting to discover what they were being intuitive about.

By the time Dido reached Scott, it was obvious that he was in a real mess. The three boys he was with were hooting with laughter, leaning against one another to keep from falling over. Dido's heart sank. Scott couldn't have picked a worse audience – Jack Farmer, Ross Williams and David Miller – Dido could see TROUBLE stamped on their foreheads.

'You all right?' she asked Scott.

'Mm!' said Scott, but he wasn't; he was humiliated. 'I've, er, just got to pop to the loo.'

He scuttled off and Dido squared up to Jack, Ross and David.

Jack was the leader. He had dark hair and sly eyes. Ross was tall and bulky. David was a runt, with wiry hair that stuck up as though he had a thousand volts running through him.

Jack said, 'Hey, is that kid your boyfriend?'

'Why?' said Dido. 'You jealous?'

This was fighting talk. Ross and David went, 'Ooooh!'

Jack twitched his shoulders.

'He's cracked,' he said. 'You want to forget about him, darling. Get yourself a real man.'

'Meaning you?' said Dido.

'You said it.'

Dido looked Jack up and down. She didn't need inseeing to spot his problem. 'You've never been out with a girl, have you, Jack?' she said.

'Haven't I?' said Jack, dropping a wink to his mates.

'Not in the real world,' said Dido. 'You're big on talking about girls and telling dirty jokes, but you're afraid you'll never find a girl who actually likes you. Don't worry, you will one day. The right girl for you is out there somewhere, but I'm not her. I've got a brain.'

'That supposed to be an insult?'

'No, it's the truth. If I ever insult you, you'll know.'

Jack tried to think of a comeback, couldn't, and resorted to curling his top lip into a sneer.

'Come on, lads,' he said to Ross and David. 'Let's go find some chicks who aren't up themselves.'

Chicks? Dido thought, What is this? Am I in some kind of time warp? Then she realised that she wasn't – but Jack was.

The sudden sound of laughter made Dido turn her head. A boy was standing a few metres away, grinning at her. His nose was longish and chiselled, his eyes were strikingly green and he had dark red, almost chestnut-coloured hair. The grin on his face was so infectious that Dido caught it and grinned back.

The boy strolled over and said, 'I like the way you handled those three just then. Good for you!'

Dido felt a blush rise from her neck to her cheeks.

'Um – thanks,' she mumbled.

'I was in Junior school with them, so I know what

they're like. Their nickname was The Terrible Trio. Ollie.'

'I'm sorry?' said Dido.

'Ollie is my name – short for Oliver.'

'Oh right – and I'm Dido Nesbit.'

'As in Mrs Nesbit, the Deputy Head?'

'Uh huh,' said Dido, bracing herself for the boy to crack a joke.

But to her surprise, Ollie said, 'You have my sympathy. My mum's a teacher too. Bummer, hey?'

'Sometimes,' said Dido. 'Does your mum teach at this school?'

'No, lucky for me. She works at Bishop Street Infants.'

A bell rang to mark the end of break.

'Better get back to the grind,' said Ollie. 'Nice talking to you, Dido. See you around.'

Dido was stunned. She hadn't been at Prince Arthur's for a full morning yet, and she'd already met two friendly faces – Scott and Ollie – and her image of herself as a loner had taken quite a dent. Maybe things were going to be different here; maybe moving hadn't been such a bad idea after all.

*

The other years came in after lunch, and the school was suddenly louder and edgier. Year Sevens were at the bottom of the heap, only to be noticed if they got in the way.

'D'you think it's always like this?' Dido asked Scott, after they had been barged through by a bunch of Year Nines.

'No, sometimes it's worse,' Scott said. 'Last Easter, two Year Ten kids killed a squirrel and nailed it to Mrs Avery's door.'

'They did *what*?'

'There was a big fuss about it in the local paper. They were both expelled. One was called John Loomis, and the other one was Billy Cooper, but everybody called him Bivco.'

Dido's magic provided her with a memory flash of the names she'd seen sprayed on the Speaking Stones.

'Bivco and Loomis,' she muttered.

'Eh?'

'Nothing. Who's Mrs Avery?'

'She used to be Deputy Head. She had a nervous breakdown and took early retirement.'

'Why did they nail a dead squirrel to her door?'

'They didn't like her. She was a bit of a dragon.'

'How come you know so much about it?'

'My brother Matt told me,' said Scott. 'He was in Year Eleven when it happened. He goes to sixth-form college now. My sister Kate told me about it too. She was in Year Seven then.'

'You've got a sister in Year Eight?'

'Yeah. My brother Chris is in the Juniors and my sister Julie's a toddler.'

'Wow, what's it like, living in such a big family?'

'Busy. You're an only child, right?'

'How did you know?'

'It shows. I'm in the middle. That shows as well.'

Dido wanted to ask how, but thought that it might be too personal; besides, her mind was busy with something else. From her researches in Shadow Magic, Dido knew of seven rituals that involved animal sacrifice. None of them was pleasant, and if Mum and Dad knew that Dido knew about them, they'd freak.

'Scott,' she said, 'that squirrel. Was it nailed to the door like this?' She spread out her arms and legs in a star shape.

'No idea,' said Scott. 'Why?'

Dido lowered her arms and brought her feet together.

'Just interested,' she said.

Scott shook his head.

'You are *seriously* strange, Dido, d'you know that?'

'All the best people are,' said Dido. 'Anyway, look who's talking.'

Because it was their first day, Year Seven went home at half past two, an hour earlier than the rest of the school. The road outside was jammed with cars, mostly driven by anxious-faced mums. On their way to the bus stop, Dido noticed Philippa Trevelyan waiting at the kerb. Philippa's head was lowered and her shoulders were slumped. A cartoonist would have drawn her with a big black cloud over her head.

'She looks kind of down,' said Scott. 'Shall we go and cheer her up?'

'I think she'd rather be left alone,' Dido said.

But Scott was right, Philippa did look down. In fact, for a potential ballet star who was about to be given a brand new laptop, she didn't look like a very happy bunny at all.

7
Miss Morgan

After her alarm clock went off next morning, Dido rolled on to her back and thought things over while she was waking up. She'd considered telling Mum and Dad the story Scott had told her about Mrs Avery, but in the end she hadn't. Mum had come home tired, frazzled and in no mood to hear that her predecessor in the Deputy Head's post might have been a victim of witchcraft. Also, Dido would have had to own up that she'd been studying Shadow Magic, and that wouldn't have gone down well. Anyhow, Dido couldn't be sure that Bivco and his friend *had* used witchcraft. Most likely it was a coincidence, an act of mindless cruelty that happened to resemble an ancient Shadow Magic ritual. She couldn't even be certain that Scott had got the facts straight.

And what about the stone circle, the charmed library book, the pentagram and the silver tabby?

Dido thought. She had a hunch that they were all linked, but she couldn't make the connection and didn't waste much time trying. She had a school day to get through and that made life complicated enough, without inventing things to make it worse.

Scott was waiting at the bus stop – or rather, Voodini was. The first thing he did was hand Dido a sealed envelope.

'What's this?' said Dido.

'A new mind-reading trick. You're going to love it. Hold the envelope tightly, so you're sure I can't tamper with it. Now, a pack of playing cards has four suits, right?'

'Right.'

'Pick two.'

'Why?'

Scott rolled his eyes.

'Just do it, will you?' he snapped.

'OK, OK! Hearts and Diamonds.'

'Which leaves?'

'Clubs and Spades.'

Scott rubbed his hands together, like something was going to plan and he was pleased. 'From Clubs and Spades, pick one.'

'Spades.'

'From the Jack, Queen, King and Ace of Spaces, pick two.'

'The Jack and the Ace.'

'Which leaves?'

'The Queen and King.'

'From the Queen and—'

'All right, I've got it already. I pick the Queen of Spades.'

'Open the envelope, please.'

Dido opened the envelope and found a playing card inside: the Queen of Spades.

Scott hugged himself gleefully.

'Ta-da!' he crowed. 'Aren't you impressed, amazed and astounded by my magical skills?'

'No.'

'Why not?'

'Because you talked me into it,' said Dido, laughing. 'You knew the Queen of Spades was in the envelope, and you made me choose it. If I chose the wrong way, you said, "Which leaves?" and if I chose the right way, you didn't say anything. Kids' stuff.'

'Oh yeah?' Scott grumbled. 'When did you get to be such a big expert on magic?'

Dido decided to try a little reverse psychology.

'As soon as I was born,' she said. 'I'm a witch from a long line of witches.'

Scott burst out laughing. 'Good one, Dido! I've never met anybody who looked less like a witch in my life.'

'Looks aren't everything, Scott. In your case, that's just as well.'

Scott responded to the insult by giving Dido a shove. She shoved him back, and suddenly her life wasn't complicated, she was just an eleven-year-old kid fooling around.

The atmosphere at school was still boisterous. Dido and Scott picked their way across the playground; Scott had to duck to avoid being concussed by a wildly kicked football. Outside C Block, Philippa was chatting to Mandy and Charlotte.

'It's really fast. I sent dozens of e-mails. My friend in Australia got on-line and we chatted for ages. I was worried about the size of the phone bill, but my parents said that they didn't mind. They say cyberspace is the future, and the best way of learning about it is to explore it while you're young. I tried to show my father how to send an e-mail, but he was useless. Why are grown-ups so slow at catching on?'

'Boy, does she know how to work an audience,' Scott said to Dido.

'Watch closely, you might pick up a few tips.'

'Maybe.'

'Mind you, she has a head start,' said Dido. 'Being pretty and having long blonde hair helps, doesn't it?'

'It does from where I'm standing.'

'Hey, back off! You're too young for girl-boy stuff.'

'I know,' said Scott, 'but I want to get some practice in before it starts for real.'

When Dido looked at Philippa again, she noticed that Mandy and Charlotte didn't exactly seem rapt any more – in fact they were showing all the signs of boredom. Mandy's face wore a long-suffering expression, and Charlotte seemed more interested in her fingernails than what Philippa was saying.

Philippa attempted to compensate by talking faster and louder, but it didn't do any good. When she paused to take a breath, Mandy said, 'You're full of it, aren't you?'

Philippa's cheeks flushed.

'What?' she said.

Mandy drew herself up to her full height and looked Philippa straight in the eye.

'Think you're so swanky, don't you? Well, if your mum and dad are so rich, how come you're at Prince Arthur's? Why didn't they send you to boarding school?'

Philippa had been wrong-footed.

'Er...my parents don't believe in private education!' she spluttered. 'They believe that everyone should have an equal chance.'

'Oh yeah?' said Mandy. 'And I think you're the biggest liar that ever walked. What d'you reckon, Charley?'

'I reckon this nail varnish I bought is rubbish!' said Charlotte. 'I only put it on last night and it's flaking already.'

Philippa's embarrassment passed the bearable mark. She rushed off, followed by the sound of Mandy and Charlotte's laughter.

'What a loser!' Mandy said scornfully.

'Yeah!' agreed Charlotte. 'You know what's sad about that girl?'

'What?'

'She's so sad!'

Scott's mouth was open in amazement.

'What was all that about?' he gasped.

'A wind-up,' said Dido. 'Mandy and Charlotte

pretended to be friends with Philippa for a day or two so they could string her along for a few cheap laughs.'

'How d'you know?'

'Because the same thing happened to me at my last school, and it wasn't nice.'

'D'you think we should find out where Philippa's gone and talk to her?'

'No. Philippa won't want to talk to anyone right now. She'll think we're trying to wind her up as well.'

'Oh,' said Scott. 'Are your thumbs all right, Dido?'

'Huh?'

'You're scratching them.'

'They're itchy.'

'Mum says that an itchy left palm means you'll soon be given money, and an itchy right palm means you'll soon be giving money to someone else. What do itchy thumbs mean?'

'It means they need scratching,' Dido said.

First lesson was Drama. Seven North lined up in the corridor outside the Drama studio, chattering and laughing until they were silenced by a voice that came from nowhere.

'Pay attention, Seven North.'

The voice was female – low and persuasive.

Dido looked around for loudspeakers and couldn't see any.

'The Drama studio is the entrance to a world where anything is possible. Enter quietly, find a place on the rows of seats and listen.'

There were no windows in the studio. The lights were low, so Dido had to find her way by touch as much as sight. The seating was banked, giving a view of the acting area, which was a black well of shadow. Above the top row of seats was the window of an empty lighting box.

Seven North waited in a hush that was only broken by excited giggles.

The giggling stopped when the voice spoke again.

'Drama is magic, and magic is the power to make others believe what you want them to believe. Actors are wizards who bewitch their audiences, and take them to places in their imaginations that they never dreamed were there.'

A spotlight came on, casting a grey-blue circle into the dark well. In the centre of the circle was what looked like a pile of old clothes.

'Watch and listen. Feel the magic.'

There was a collective gasp as the clothes twitched, rose up like a column of smoke and turned into a young woman dressed in grey robes. Her long black hair flowed over her shoulders. She was attractive rather than pretty, with a strong, slightly crooked nose, a wide mouth and pale eyes that glittered in the spotlight.

Something in the air crackled like electricity. Dido felt as though she'd been stapled to her seat. She couldn't take her eyes off the young woman.

The wide mouth shaped itself into a satisfied smile.

She knows just what she's doing, Dido thought.

'Welcome, Seven North,' the young woman said. 'I am your Drama teacher. My name is Miss Morgan.'

All the lights came on; whatever had been holding Seven North relaxed its grip. Someone began to clap, and then everybody joined in. Miss Morgan bowed, partly mocking herself, partly accepting her due.

They played Wink-Murder, and a word game where they stood in a circle and made up a long, rambling sentence that grew more and more ridiculous. That was followed by a trust game, in groups of two and three: instructing a blindfolded partner around an obstacle course, or positioning them to sit down safely on a chair that they couldn't see.

Miss Morgan seemed to be everywhere. When Jack, Ross and David started mucking about, Miss

Morgan told them off. They were stunned, because she was on the other side of the studio with her back turned to them.

The lesson raced by, and when the bell rang there were loud groans of disappointment.

On the way to History, Dido said, 'Well that was different, wasn't it?'

'Uh huh,' said Scott.

'Miss Morgan certainly grabs your attention, doesn't she?'

'Uh huh.'

Scott sounded peculiar. Dido peered at him and saw that his face was stretched into a soppy grin.

'What's the matter with you?' she said.

'I think I just fell in love.'

'Who with?'

'Miss Morgan. She's drop-dead gorgeous.'

'But she's a teacher!'

'I don't care. I think she's perfect. Miss Morgan is a babe!'

And Scott wasn't the only one who thought so. For the rest of the day, Miss Morgan was the main topic of conversation.

Dido didn't get it: it had been a good lesson, but not *that* good. She was on her own though. The rest of Seven North were head-over-heels. Miss Morgan had completely charmed them, and Dido began to wonder if Miss Morgan had just used charm, or *a* charm.

Mum came in at six, looking whacked. She sagged against the kitchen doorway and watched glassily as Dad and Dido prepared dinner.

'How was today?' Dad asked.

'Hellish,' said Mum. 'I had a confrontation with a Year Ten girl about the length of her skirt. It was right up to—' Mum broke off with a sigh. 'I don't want to talk about it. What kind of day did you have, Dido?'

'Weird,' said Dido. 'We had our first Drama lesson with Miss Morgan this morning, and she—'

'Oh, Alice Morgan,' Mum said. 'The school could do with more teachers like her. D'you know, she's the only member of staff who's offered me any sympathy? I think we're going to be good mates. I feel as if I've known her for years. I must invite her over for a meal some time.'

'Is she a looker?' said Dad.

'She's stunning.'

'How about inviting her over tomorrow?'

Mum laughed.

Dido didn't; there was something mysterious about Miss Morgan, and Dido wanted to know if it was a nice mysterious or a nasty mysterious before any dinner invitations went out.

8
Runner in the Rain

Dido settled into a routine. As she learned her way around the school and her teachers, she didn't notice how time seemed to speed up, until suddenly she found herself waiting to catch the bus home on Friday afternoon.

'Hey, Scott, we made it!' Dido said.

Scott was trying to undo a complicated knot in a piece of string, without much success.

'Made what?' he said.

'We got through our first week at Prince Arthur's. We haven't been beaten up, mugged or put into detention. This calls for a celebration.'

'What kind of celebration?'

'Why don't we meet up for a burger in town tomorrow afternoon? You can show me the sights.'

The corners of Scott's mouth turned down.

'I can't,' he said. 'Mum works on Saturday, so does

Matt. Kate and I have to look after Julie and do the housework. I dust and hoover, Kate does the washing.'

Without thinking, Dido said, 'Doesn't your dad help out, or is he at work too?' and immediately realised that she shouldn't have asked.

Scott's face was expressionless, and when he spoke his voice was expressionless too.

'Mum and Dad split up at Christmas,' he said.

Dido could have bitten off her tongue.

'I'm sorry,' she said.

'That's OK. Actually, it's easier now Dad's left. He and Mum aren't screaming at each other all the time. He moved to London. We see him every once in a while.'

Dido sensed that Scott wasn't as cool about it as he was making out, and said, 'Hey, you don't have to tell me. If it's painful to talk about—'

'I'd rather tell you myself than have you hear it from somebody else,' Scott said. 'Dad was having an affair and Mum found out. It was like something out of a soap opera, only the acting was better. The worst part is Julie. She keeps asking when Dad's coming home. She's too young to understand what's going on.'

'And do you?'

'Do I what?'

'Understand what's going on.'

Scott shrugged.

'I'm getting there,' he said. 'It was hard at first. I was really angry with Dad, but then Mum explained that...well, I guess I'd better keep that part private.'

Dido admired Scott. Behind all his bad jokes and klutzy conjuring tricks, he was coping with a difficult situation and managing not to feel bitter about it.

'Thanks,' said Dido.

'For?'

'Trusting me.'

'Thanks for being there for me to trust. I guess that makes us friends, right? Friends tell each other stuff, don't they?'

'Yes they do.' Suddenly Dido made a decision. She knew she was taking a risk, but she also knew that she had to: if trust didn't work both ways in a friendship, it wasn't worth having. She took a deep breath. 'Scott, remember I told you I was a witch and you thought that I was joking? Well I wasn't. It was for real.'

Scott laughed long and loud, using the laughter as a safety valve. He blotted tears from his eyes with the sleeve of his shirt.

'That's one of the things I like about you, Dido,' he said. 'You always know the right thing to say.'

So much for trust, thought Dido. Some days you can't even *give* the truth away.

'And what else?' she said.

'Huh?'

'You said it was one of the things you like about me, so what are the others?'

Scott thought for a while, then said, 'You know Wednesday lunchtime, when you drank that can of Coke and burped?'

'Y-e-e-s.'

'It was pretty impressive. I never heard a girl burp like that before.'

'No?' said Dido. 'You ought to hear me after I've eaten baked beans!'

On Saturday morning, Mum gave up being Mrs Nesbit, Deputy Head. All week long she'd made decisions for other people, been positive and dynamic; now her time was her own she drifted like a jellyfish in a current, sipping coffee in the kitchen while Dad buzzed around the cupboards, making a shopping list.

'How are we for loo rolls, Faye?'

'Sorry?'

'Loo rolls? You know, the things you use to—?'

'Not sure. I'll go and check.'

'I'll go and check. You'll get to the bathroom and forget what you're doing there.'

As Dad climbed the stairs, he met Dido coming down.

'Your mother's in airhead mode,' he warned. 'Be gentle with her. She needs to chill.'

'Da-ad! I wish you wouldn't say that.'

'What?'

'Chill. It's so last century.'

'Well, whatever the word is, it's what your mother needs, OK?'

When Dido entered the kitchen, Mum gave her a good-morning smile.

'Want some toast?' Mum said.

'I can do my own, thanks,' said Dido.

'Your father and I are going to the supermarket after breakfast. Would you like to come with us?'

Dido pulled a face.

'*Like?*' she said. 'Would I *like* to go to the supermarket? What's likeable about it? I'd rather stay at home.'

'If you stay at home, what will you do?'

'I don't know – watch TV, take a walk and explore the neighbourhood?'

Mum frowned.

'You won't talk to any strange men, will you?' she said.

'Honestly, Mum. What d'you take me for?'

'A young girl.'

'But I'm not exactly helpless, am I? I've got resources I can draw on if I have to take care of myself. Anyway, going shopping with you and Dad sucks. You always have one of those under-the-breath rows.'

'We always kiss and make up though.'

'Yeah, usually in the middle of an aisle. I mean, how embarrassing is that?'

Cosmo caused a distraction by jumping on to the work surface and head-butting Dido's arm, while mewing busily.

'Yes, they'll remember the cat food,' Dido said. 'I'll make sure they put it at the top of the list. And no, they won't buy semi-skimmed milk again.'

Mum laughed. 'You and that cat! Anyone would think you understand each other.'

'We do,' said Dido. 'So, are you going to force me to go to the supermarket now you know I don't want to?'

'That's blatant manipulation.'

'Uh huh. Did it work?'

'I'm worried about the neighbours,' Mum said. 'If they see you wandering the streets on your own, they'll think we don't care about you, and that won't go down very well at school, will it?'

Line-drawing time! Dido thought. She said, 'Mum, is the Deputy Headship a job, or is it something that's going to rule our lives?'

Mum sighed and screwed her mouth to one side.

'Bull's-eye!' thought Dido.

'If you weren't my own daughter,' Mum said, 'I'd say that you just used a persuasion spell on me.'

'As if. You'd suss me straightaway.'

'Normally I would, but I'm not so sure at the moment. School's taken a lot out of me. I should spend an hour meditating in the sanctuary this afternoon, to get back in touch with myself.'

Dido grinned.

'*Get back in touch with yourself, man!*' she drawled. 'That sounds really New Age hippy-drippy.'

'Well it would, wouldn't it?' said Mum. 'Where d'you think they pinched all their ideas from?'

*

Dido watched children's TV, zapping between channels until she couldn't stand it any longer, which took about two minutes. It was all junk cartoons, dumb competitions, rubber puppets, hyperactive presenters who cackled at their own jokes; exactly the same on every station. The producers of the shows hadn't lost any sleep over the quality of their material, and they certainly didn't over-estimate the intelligence of their audience.

Dido turned off the TV, went to glance out of the window, walked into the hall and noticed that she was pacing. Something was making her restless; she stopped and concentrated.

There it was again: a snagging feeling, like a hangnail catching on wool. Dido relaxed into inseeing, and felt her body go weightless as her mind spread out like water spilled on a tablecloth. Her consciousness passed through the walls and into the streets.

She heard voices: a mother scolding a child; an angry pensioner complaining about the prices of items in a shop; a young couple arguing. More voices joined them, merging into a babble of unhappiness. Then Dido's magic homed in on a single voice – a young girl's voice.

'They don't care about me! No one cares about me! It wouldn't matter to them if I was alive or dead. They'd be better off without me!'

Dido snapped back inside herself and noticed that her thumbs were tingling. Her magic was trying to tell her something.

'What?' she whispered.

The magic wouldn't say, but Dido knew that her thumbs would give her no peace until she found out what was bothering them. She put on a jacket, slipped a key in her pocket and left the house.

The sky was inky black; the air smelled of rain. Dido followed her thumbs. It was a bit like treasure hunting, only instead of saying, 'warmer' or 'colder', Dido's thumbs got itchier when she took a wrong turning. They led her to Stanstowe Road, the main route into town. By now it was so dark that all the cars had their headlights on.

A cold raindrop splashed on to the tip of Dido's nose and she dived for the nearest available cover, the bus shelter where she met Scott every morning.

The rain belted down, bouncing off the pavement. Dido twisted sideways to avoid the water cascading off the roof of the shelter, and caught her breath.

Ten metres away, a young girl was running, head

down, the hood of her jacket pulled over her face. As Dido watched, a lightning bolt crackled across the sky, startling the girl so that she stumbled and fell, landing heavily on the pavement.

Dido darted out of the shelter, rushed over and said, 'You OK?'

The girl looked up. It was Philippa Trevelyan, her mouth twisted in a pained grimace.

'Kind of,' she said.

Dido reached out to help Philippa to her feet. When Philippa took Dido's hand, Dido felt a jolt like an electric shock.

Dido's thumbs had led her to Philippa because it was Philippa's voice she'd heard while she was inseeing. Philippa was in some kind of mess.

And then they were both in a mess. A passing transporter lorry drove through the deep pool that had formed over a blocked drain, and drenched them both with a sheet of dirty water.

9
Heart-to-Heart

Philippa gazed down at herself in dismay. Her jeans were black, and when she bent her knees, water oozed out of the denim.

Dido burst out laughing.

'What's so funny?' Philippa asked.

'We are!' Dido gurgled. 'There's getting wet, and then there's getting really wet, but we are *ridiculously* wet!'

Philippa laughed too. 'We *are* wet, aren't we?' she said.

'If we were any wetter, we'd grow gills.'

Despite Philippa's film-star grin, her eyes were dark and guarded.

She's tighter than the packaging on a supermarket sandwich, Dido thought.

Philippa flapped her arms and said, 'Well, I suppose I'd better—'

Dido had a split second to make up her mind. She could let Philippa go on her way, or keep her talking and find out more about why magic had brought them together.

'Philippa,' Dido said, 'my house isn't far from here. Why don't you come back with me and get warmed up and dry?'

'U-u-m.'

'Hot chocolate,' said Dido. 'With marshmallow bits.'

She added a coaxing spell. Like all other Light Magic spells, it was made from what Dido knew. Images of things being persuaded came into her mind – a piece of string being dangled in front of a kitten, a magnet picking up a needle – and she felt her magic catch the mood of the images.

'Thanks,' said Philippa. 'You're sure it's not too much trouble?'

'No trouble,' Dido said.

Philippa was in a quiet sort of mood, so on the way to Mistletoe Lane, Dido did the talking for them both. She rabbited on about the move, the new house, the old house, school, anything she could think of. At the same time, she checked Philippa out with inseeing. Philippa was enveloped by a thin silvery glow, like the light in the sky before sunrise. It was only a momentary contact, but Dido sensed grief, anger and confusion. Philippa needed help to make sense of her emotions, and all Dido's instincts told her that she was just the Light Witch for the job.

When they reached the house, Dido's practical side kicked in. She took Philippa through to the kitchen, gave her a clean towel to dry her hair and made two mugs of chocolate.

Philippa clutched her mug in both hands.

'This is really kind of you,' she said between sips.

'Forget it. What were you doing on Stanstowe Road anyway – you live near the school, don't you?'

Philippa avoided Dido's eye contact.

'I was taking a walk,' she said. 'I needed to be on my own, away from my family, you know?'

Dido suddenly found herself casting a persuasion spell that made itself up from a dog gazing longingly at its lead, a little girl nagging her mother in the toy section of a department store and the sound of Cosmo asking to be fed. Dido hadn't been expecting the spell, and it was a little shabby around the edges because she was getting tired. Two sessions of inseeing and two spells in the space of half an hour was pushing things a bit, and Dido felt as if she'd just finished a two-hundred metre sprint.

The spell's effect was instant. Philippa sighed and said, 'Look, Dido, there's something you should know about me. All that stuff I come out with in school, like the laptop and the ballet classes? None of it's true. I used to go to ballet classes because my mother made me, but—' Philippa took a deep breath, fighting back tears. 'Mum was killed in a car accident two years ago. After she died it was just me, Dad and my kid brother, Tom. We helped one another to get through the bad times, and for a while we managed fine. Then six months ago Dad started seeing someone, and I think it's serious. I think he wants to get married again, and I hate the idea. It's like he wants to rub out Mum's memory.' The persuasion spell began to wear off. Philippa became conscious of how much she'd revealed about herself, and said, 'You won't tell anyone at school about this, will you?'

'Hey,' said Dido. 'I don't do gossip.'

Philippa relaxed.

'I didn't think so,' she said. 'You know what I thought the first time I saw you?'

'Who's the mess?' Dido suggested.

Philippa smiled weakly. 'No, I thought you were someone it would be good to have as a friend.' She laughed to cover her embarrassment. 'I don't know why, it was like a voice in my head whispered it to me.'

Or my magic wanted us to be friends for some reason, thought Dido. She said, 'Did your mum love your dad?'

'Of course!' Philippa gasped, taken aback by Dido's directness.

'Then she would've wanted him to be happy, wouldn't she? She'd be glad that he's found someone new.'

'I'm not.'

'That's your problem, not his. You have to find a way of joining in with his happiness instead of fighting it.'

'I'm not going to forget about Mum!' Philippa said defiantly.

'Who said you would? Your mum's a part of you. As long as you're alive, a bit of her is still alive too.'

Philippa smiled: it was only a small smile, but it was genuine.

'I never thought about it that way before,' she said. 'How d'you get to be so wise, Dido?' she joked.

'Me?' said Dido. 'I'm an old, wise woman trapped in a young girl's body.'

Which, as it turned out, was closer to the truth than Dido realised.

Philippa laughed, glanced at her watch and scowled.

'I have to go now,' she said. 'I owe you one, Dido. I'll pay you back some time.'

Dido glanced out of the kitchen window; the storm had blown itself out and the sun was shining.

'No time like the present,' she said. 'The weather's cleared up. What are you doing this afternoon?'

'Nothing much – why?'

'Want to meet me in town later and show me around?'

'Sure...if you don't mind other people seeing you with a terrible liar.'

'I don't think you're a terrible liar,' said Dido. 'From what I've seen, you lie really well! I'll meet you outside the Town Hall at half two, OK?'

Philippa beamed.

'OK,' she said.

Mum and Dad arrived home twenty minutes after Philippa left. Mum peered suspiciously at Dido and said, 'What have you been up to?'

'All kinds of exciting stuff,' Dido said. 'I watched

telly, then I took a walk. I bumped into this girl from my form. We got caught in the rain, so I brought her back here for a hot drink. She wants me to meet her in town later.'

'Town?' Mum said sharply.

'Yeah, you know, that place with all the shops and people?'

Mum didn't seem too keen.

'Which girl?' she said.

'Philippa Trevelyan.'

'Is she in Seven North?'

'Yes.'

'All right then,' Mum said reluctantly. 'But I want you back by six. You're looking worn out. I hope getting wet hasn't given you a cold.'

'It hasn't.'

'Have you been casting spells? You know that I don't like you to experiment without supervision.'

'Would I do something like that?' said Dido, as innocently as she could manage.

'Yes.'

Dad staggered in, laden with shopping bags.

'Don't mind me,' he said. 'I can manage. Another ten trips to the car ought to do it.'

Dido said, 'Isn't there a spell you could use so you

don't have to go back and forth so much?'

'Yes,' said Dad. 'It's called, "Would someone please give me a hand?"'

Dido set out for town after lunch. Mum stood at the lounge window and watched until Dido disappeared at the end of the street. Dad came into the room and caught her watching.

'Worried?' he said.

'I can't help it. She's still just a kid.'

'She's growing up, Faye. Children of eleven know a lot more than we did at their age.'

'That's one of the things that worries me.'

Dad crossed the room and wrapped his arms around Mum.

'Before you know it, she'll be a stroppy teenager,' he said. 'We'll have to let her go eventually.'

'I know, but so much depends upon her. D'you think we should—?'

'What?'

'Explain the situation to her. Then she'd know what was at stake. It might make her more cautious.'

'And it might be too much too soon,' said Dad. 'She might see it as a burden rather than a responsibility. As you said, she's still a kid. Let her enjoy it while she can.'

'You're right,' Mum said with a sigh. 'Maybe I'm being an over-protective mother hen. I should go down to the sanctuary to meditate for an hour or so.'

'To meditate, or to pray for guidance?'

'Both,' said Mum.

10
The Trap

Philippa was waiting outside the Town Hall, on a bench near the statue of Queen Victoria. She waved when she saw Dido and the sunlight caught her fair hair, momentarily turning her into an angel. She looked much happier, as if talking to Dido had helped her to let go of something heavy that she'd been lugging around.

Is that it? Dido thought. Is that why my magic drew us together, to tell me that this is the way to go – pre-teen counselling? Will I wind up writing an Ask Dido column in a mag like *Glitz Girlz*?

It seemed a depressing prospect; Dido had enough problems of her own to sort out, without taking on other people's.

Dido sat down next to Philippa.

'Dad put up my clothing allowance today,' Philippa declared.

'Oh?' said Dido.

'He thinks it's important for someone my age to dress fashionably,' Philippa said brightly. 'He's quite generous about some things. He says—'

'Philippa,' Dido said gently, 'no more lying, OK? You tried it out with Mandy and Charlotte. It didn't work on them, and it's not going to work on me.'

Philippa seemed to deflate.

'You're right,' she said. 'It's an awful habit and I have to stop. I can't believe that I told lies to impress Mandy Dean and Charlotte Barnes. I mean – how pathetic is that? I'd rather talk to you than them.'

'Then tell the truth while you're doing it.'

'Agreed,' said Philippa. 'Oh, by the way, I meant to ask you something this morning, but I forgot.'

'Ask away,' Dido said.

'You won't be offended, will you?'

'I'll be offended if you offend me, but I can't tell in advance.'

'Well, the thing is, you know that boy you hang around with, Scott Pink? Is he your boyfriend?'

Dido laughed. 'No way!' she said. 'Scott's a friend. On the first day at school he was like a limpet who figured I'd make a good rock, and now he's stuck to me.'

'Not stuck *on* you then?'

'Nah!'

'He's a bit...er...strange, isn't he?'

'Most people are, when you get to know them,' said Dido. 'Normal people are the really strange ones.'

'You like boys?'

'They're OK when they're not in a gang.'

'I like boys,' Philippa said dreamily. 'Older boys, you know, fifteen or sixteen? They're more...'

'Old?' Dido said.

'Mature. My dad says I'm too young to date anyone yet, but I don't think eleven and three-quarters is too young, do you?'

'That would depend on the kind of date,' said Dido. She could tell that Philippa was off again, not lying but fantasising. Dido doubted if Philippa had been asked out on a date yet, but guessed that it wouldn't be too long before she was.

'D'you ever try to imagine what your super-special someone looks like?' Philippa said.

'No,' said Dido. 'I'd rather he came as a surprise. Look, Philippa, this is a comfortable bench and everything, but if you're going to show me around, shouldn't we go somewhere?'

'Where would you like to go?'

'You tell me – you're the guide.'

Philippa stood up.

'There's only one place to start,' she said. 'The Pentacle. After you've been there, the rest of town is pretty much a let-down.'

Dido's thumbs prickled.

Knock it off, guys! she said to them in her head. What can go wrong in the middle of a shopping mall on a Saturday afternoon?

People were streaming in and out of The Pentacle's main entrance, crossing over the concrete bridge that spanned a narrow stream. High on the wall above the automatic glass doors was an engraved stone plaque.

ADVANCE THROUGH THE GATEWAY
INTO THE HALLS OF THE FUTURE.
SIR EDWIN LANGLEY-DAVIS

Him again! thought Dido, and said, 'Hey, Philippa, who's Sir Edwin Langley-Davis?'

'Some Victorian factory owner,' said Philippa. 'The park at the back of the Town Hall is named after him, and there's a portrait of him in the museum. Why d'you want to know?'

'I read something by him in an archaeology book.'

'Archaeology book?' Philippa boggled. 'Come on, Dido. You definitely need some retail therapy. The only reading you have to do is price tags.'

The mall was heaving and the sound level was almost intolerable. The roof – a tent of steel and plate glass – reflected back every voice and every snatch of shop muzak. There were pentagrams everywhere: on posters, frosted on to the glass of shop doors, set in mosaics on the floors. Signs fixed to support pillars read, Welcome to an Exciting New Shopping Experience, but nobody seemed particularly excited. Most of the crowd shuffled along dead-eyed, and Dido wondered if they'd been churned out by a zombie factory.

'Loud, isn't it?' she said.

'Think so?' said Philippa. 'Certainly has a buzz, doesn't it?'

'I'd call it more of a scream myself.'

Philippa trawled around clothes shops, picking out outfits for herself. Her taste was inclined towards the flashy end of the fashion spectrum – skimpy satin tops in bright colours, hipster flares with sparkly stuff stuck on the legs. It was kind of fun to be with

Philippa and act girly for a change, so Dido said, 'Wow!' at Philippa's more outrageous selections, and pretended to drool. Philippa wasn't actually about to buy anything, and there was no harm in looking.

After forty-five minutes of pink sequins and diamante, Dido was glammed-out; so when Philippa said, 'That's about it for clothes,' Dido felt relieved. Then Philippa went on, 'Time to hit HMV!'

'Whoa, slow down, Philippa,' said Dido. 'I could really use a break and something to drink. Is there anywhere we can grab a quick juice?'

Philippa bobbed her head from side to side.

'There's Hasta La Vista, Luigi's or Chez Cherie's,' she said. 'There's even a coffee bar in Springer's bookshop, but I warn you, it isn't the coolest place in town.'

'I don't mind about cool, as long as they serve wet stuff in glasses, and a bookshop sounds nice.'

Springer's was on the ground floor, in between a Warner Brothers store and a nail bar. When Dido crossed the threshold, the bustling chaos of the mall was replaced by an atmosphere of quiet calm. There was just a handful of customers, searching the bookshelves to the strains of gentle classical music. Dido loved bookshops, and as she walked through

Springer's she was impressed by the range of books on offer. She put the shop on top of her revisit list, especially after she caught a tantalising glimpse of the size of the Occult section.

In the coffee bar, Philippa bought herself a Coke and insisted on paying for Dido's orange juice. Dido looked around for somewhere to sit and saw that she was spoiled for choice. Just a single table was occupied, and one of the two occupants was beckoning her over. It was Ollie, seated opposite a sullen-looking older boy with short bleached hair.

'You know him?' said Philippa.

'Slightly,' Dido said. 'He's in our year at Prince Arthur's. Shall we go over there?'

'Sure!' said Philippa, staring hard at the blond boy.

Ollie welcomed Dido the way a drowning sailor welcomes a lifeboat. The sulky boy turned out to be Ollie's older brother Steve. When Ollie introduced Dido and Philippa, Steve acknowledged them by lifting his eyebrows a millimetre and saying, 'You'll be OK if I leave you with your friends, won't you, Ollie? I want to check out the new DVDs in Virgin. Meet you on the bridge in half an hour, yeah?'

He stood and walked out of the shop, without waiting for Ollie to reply.

Dido sensed Ollie's awkwardness and said, 'Is it something we did?'

'No,' said Ollie. 'Mum and Dad lumbered him with taking me shopping for some new shoes. Steve's worried we might run into his mates and they'll take the mickey out of him. He and I don't get along too well.'

'It's the same with me and my brother,' Philippa chipped in. 'He's nine, and he's a real pain.'

And all at once she and Ollie were deep in a conversation about what they had to put up with from their respective brothers. Since she didn't have anything to contribute, Dido let her eyes and her attention wander.

The windows of the coffee bar looked out over the main concourse of the mall to the big escalators that ran up and down between the floors. Three young lads were mucking around on the up escalator, pulling and pushing one another and throwing mock punches. Dido instantly recognised them – Jack, Ross and David, The Terrible Trio. They were having their own private version of fun, but didn't realise just how stupid they were being. The escalator was packed, and if one of the trio slipped, they'd knock somebody over and start a chain reaction that would result in a serious accident.

Dido's inseeing eye opened with a suddenness that took her by surprise. It zoomed in on Jack, giving her a close-up view of what he was carrying on his back – a mischief spell, a horrible thing, like a cross between a bat and a hedgehog. It had its black twiggy legs wrapped around Jack's neck; its leathery wings were folded, but its spines bristled with pleasure.

Knowing that if she didn't do something, the Accident and Emergency unit of the local hospital would have broken arms and legs to deal with, Dido chanced an unlocking spell that was filled with doors swinging open, flowers unfolding their petals and pack ice splitting into jagged plates. Dido was still tired from her morning's magic, and the strain of the spell made her head throb.

The mischief spell felt Dido's magic and swivelled its head in an attempt to trace the source.

Then something went badly wrong. A force like a gigantic fist seized Dido and tore her out of the world. The coffee shop fell away at incredible speed, dwindling to a tiny point of light that winked out.

Dido tried to break free, but the force was too

strong and urged her forwards. She was in a dark place, surrounded by trees. She heard the wind sighing through their branches, smelled pine resin and woodsmoke. Between the trunks of the trees was an orange glimmer.

Dido staggered out of the trees into a place she recognised – the circle of stones on the top of Stanstowe Hill – but the circle was in a different time. The stones were cleaner and sharper-edged. To her left, where the street lamps of Stanstowe should have been shining, was blackness.

A fire burned at the centre of the circle; the stones seemed to twitch in the shifting light. Just beyond the fire stood a figure, and something about it made Dido afraid.

Then a chant drifted through the air.

'*Palecorum alnech la,*
Saletarum detha na…'

Dido realised with a shudder that she was listening to the sound of Shadow Magic. Her fear rose into terror. Soon she would be at the middle of the circle, and she knew that when the lurking figure saw her clearly, there would be no escape. The mischief spell that bound Jack had been booby-trapped, and Dido had been caught by it. She made a last desperate effort, flung out a charm of fangs, thorns and broken glass, screamed out the Goddess's name and—

The coffee bar sprang up around her. Philippa and Ollie were staring at her, gobsmacked.

Dido panicked. Had Ollie and Philippa seen anything that might betray her? How much had she given away?

'Dido, are you feeling all right?' said Ollie. 'Your face has gone white.'

Dido did some quick thinking and cupped a hand over her left ear.

'It's nothing,' she said. 'My ear got infected over the summer holidays and it hasn't cleared up yet. I still get these giddy turns.'

Philippa smiled sympathetically, but Ollie frowned, as if he didn't quite buy Dido's story.

Dido didn't worry about what Ollie thought, she had other things on her mind. She'd seen mischief spells before. Light Witches cast them to play practical jokes, and the spells were never booby-trapped. The spell she'd just dealt with had been different: uglier, stronger and more vicious, and Shadow Magic had definitely been involved. All the odd happenings, that Dido had noticed since the move, clicked together and made a pattern.

There was a distinct possibility that, somewhere in Stanstowe, a Shadowmaster was at work.

11
Personal

On the bus ride home, Dido had to face some tough decisions. Up until now, her investigations into Shadow Magic had been like a game that was fun because she knew that she was doing something her parents disapproved of; but playtime was over. Her brush with the Stanstowe Shadowmaster, if there *was* a Stanstowe Shadowmaster, had come within a hair's breadth of ending in total disaster, and it had shaken her badly. She'd gone in way over her head, and the helplessness of being in the grip of Shadow Magic was a sensation that she didn't want to repeat. Like it or not, she needed her parents' help, and that meant coming clean to them about her secret studies too.

Mum would go ballistic and ground her for at least a month, but Dad's reaction would be worse. He'd be quietly disappointed with Dido, and make her feel as though she'd let him down. Dido hated it when her father laid a guilt trip on her, particularly when she deserved it. Mum and Dad had been right and she'd been wrong – Shadow Magic was something she should have left well alone, but she hadn't been able to resist it. *Dabbling*, Mum called it, but Dido had never been one for dabbling; when she got involved with something, she got stuck in right up to her elbows.

Dad was in the lounge when Dido got back. He was on the sofa, busily clacking away at his laptop, and he didn't look up when Dido entered the room.

'Where's Mum?' Dido asked.

'Meditating in the sanctuary,' said Dad. 'She's been there all afternoon.'

'What are you doing?'

'Playing a computer game so I can write a review of it.'

The game's packaging was on the floor, near Dad's feet. Dido read the title upside down, Hyperspace Racers.

'You get paid for playing games?' she said.

Dad shot Dido a sour glance. 'This is work, Dido,' he said, looking back at the screen. 'I'm not doing it for fun. Ha! Gotcha! Eat my intergalactic dust, loser!'

'Is it any good?'

'Quietly addictive. Damn!' The computer played a mocking tune; Dad scribbled something on to a notepad.

Dido judged that a little beating about the bush was in order.

'Dad,' she said, 'what's the deal with Light Witches and Shadowmasters? Is it a live-and-let-live thing, or are they sworn enemies, or what?'

Dad sighed, put down his notepad and closed the lid of the laptop.

'Your mother doesn't like you to talk about things like this,' he said.

'I know she doesn't, but how about you? Do you think I ought to be kept in the dark and treated like a baby?'

Dido could tell she'd scored a direct hit, because Dad shifted position and cleared his throat.

'Not a word to your mother, OK?' he said furtively.

'You've got it.'

'Basically, Light Witches and Shadowmasters avoid one another as much as possible. Shadowmasters are fiercely territorial and they resent other witches muscling in on their patch.'

So far, Dad hadn't told Dido anything she didn't

already know, so she pushed him a bit further.

'What do they do about it?' she said.

'They hunt them down.'

'And?'

Dad had reached the edge of what he was prepared to divulge, and from the way he was twitching, it seemed an uncomfortable place to be.

'Dido, why are you asking me these questions?'

'Because you'll answer them and Mum won't.'

'That's not what I meant, and you know it.'

Here comes the crunch, thought Dido, but the moment she opened her mouth to tell Dad what had happened in The Pentacle, a vivid image leapt into her mind.

She was standing in front of a vast wall of massive stone blocks. It stretched out either side of her as far as her eyes could see and the top was so high that it was wreathed with clouds. At first she thought the wall had something to do with the booby-trapped mischief spell, that it was a barrier erected by the Shadowmaster, but somehow it didn't give her the feeling of Shadow Magic. The stone blocks were warm to the touch, almost welcoming, and it dawned on Dido that the wall was protecting her, not shutting her out. Her magic was telling her to keep quiet.

'I just wanted to find out, that's all,' she said.

'I'm pleased you're showing an interest in magic, but curiosity isn't always a good thing,' said Dad. 'The path of magic isn't straight, it twists and turns like a corkscrew and it's easy to get lost. I wouldn't want that to happen to you.'

'No worries, Pops!'

Dad winced.

'Don't call me Pops, Dido,' he said. 'It's what I used to call my grandad.'

'I get the message, Daddykins.'

Dad grumbled under his breath and returned to the computer game.

Late that night, Dido had a dream. She was struggling upstairs with a suitcase that weighed a tonne, but no matter how far she climbed, there were always more stairs. When she looked upwards, she could see them multiplying, the upstairs landing growing more and more distant.

Dido decided to give up and turned to go down, but the hallway had turned into a restaurant. The restaurant tables were spread with linen cloths, and in the middle of each cloth stood a silver candlestick supporting a black candle. The customers in the restaurant were in full evening dress, and they were all staring at her.

'Stop looking at me like that!' she protested. 'If everything keeps changing, how can I get to where I'm supposed to go?'

To Dido's disgust, a large, winged insect appeared out of nowhere. It hovered in front of Dido's face, tickling her bottom lip with its long, dangling legs, and then it stung her.

Dido woke up and found that Cosmo was dabbing at her bottom lip with a front paw whose claws were slightly extended.

'Whassat?' mumbled Dido, fuddled with sleep.

Cosmo responded by tramping over the bed, wauling urgently.

Dido came fully awake.

'Cut it out, Cosmo!' she said. 'You'll wake Mum and Dad.'

But Cosmo wouldn't cut it out. She jumped down, sat facing the wall at the foot of the bed and wauled even louder.

Dido didn't have to be fluent in Cat to understand that Cosmo was giving her a warning about something. She rolled out of bed and went to investigate.

'What is it, Cosmo?'

'W-a-a-l-l!' howled Cosmo. 'W-a-a-l-l!'

Dido peered. A patch of wall was glowing dimly, like the hands of a luminous watch. The pattern on the wallpaper was moving, curling round on itself and forming a spiral. As Dido watched, the pattern gathered itself into a shape and the wall suddenly bulged towards her, as though it were made of elastic. Something was pushing at it, trying to get in. Dido saw the outline of a shoulder and an arm. The wall made a screeching, creaking sound, like fingertips rubbing over a balloon.

A wave of fear surged through Dido, but she knew that if she panicked, she was lost. She held back the fear and, concentrating hard, began to hum the song she'd used to charm the mouse from hiding, but reversed the order of the notes to make it repulsive rather than attractive. A spell made itself up in her head; she saw guillotine blades rattling downwards, icicles dropping off eaves, ropes parting.

The swirling pattern went grainy, and flickered like the picture on a badly tuned TV. The wall snapped back flat, and Dido's bedroom was filled with the stale scent of withered flowers.

Cosmo miaowed.

'Too right, that was close!' Dido agreed. 'Thanks for waking me.'

Cosmo purred.

'Flattery will get you nowhere,' said Dido, toughing it out to conceal how scared she was. 'I'm not going to feed you at this time of night, but I'll give you turkey treats in the morning, deal?'

Cosmo sprang on to the bed and curled up.

Dido clambered under her duvet and lay gazing at the ceiling. The shock of what had just happened left her arms and legs trembling. She felt as if she had a videotape inside her, and it had run off its spool. Dido tried to relax, and worked on teasing out the tangles.

When she was calmer and the trembling had stopped, Dido got angry. 'That was a mistake, Shadowmaster,' she whispered to the darkness. 'Messing around with time and dragging me off to the circle is one thing, but trying to break into my bedroom is *personal*!'

12
At the Centre

The downside of being an eleven-year-old witch was the homework. Dido had a double dose: the French, English, Maths and Science she did for school, and the exercises in magic with Mum and Dad. It meant slogging away at school work all Sunday morning to free up the afternoon for magic lessons.

After lunch, Dido and her father went down the garden to the sanctuary. Dido breezed in, but Dad waited outside.

'Aren't we forgetting something?' he said.

'What?'

'You have to ask the Goddess's permission for me to enter.'

'Why?'

'Because that's the tradition.'

Dido sighed. 'And why is it a tradition again?'

'It's a sign of respect. I'm a mere male, so the

Goddess has to decide if I'm worthy of entry to her sanctuary.'

'Isn't that sexist?'

'Maybe, but if I offend her I'll have four weeks of bad spells, so ask her.'

Dido turned to the statue and said, 'Is it cool for my dad to come in?'

'Properly!' said Dad.

Dido lowered her head. 'Goddess, please allow my father beneath the roof of your holy shrine.'

'That was better,' said Dad, crossing the threshold. 'Now let's get down to business. Your mother mentioned that you've been having some trouble with your animal charming.'

'I have not! Remember that mouse I charmed our first morning here? I didn't have any trouble with that, did I?'

'In that case, you won't mind showing me, will you?'

For the next half hour, Dido charmed woodlice, slugs and a squirrel. Then Dad made her go over holding spells and unlocking spells until Dido was thoroughly fed up.

'When do I get to learn something new?' she grumbled.

'When you've mastered the simple skills,' said Dad. 'Magic should happen without thought, as naturally as breathing. It's a part of you. Once you're in harmony with it, you'll be ready to go deeper.'

'Is it the same with Shadow Magic?'

Dad rolled his eyes.

'You don't let up, do you?' he said.

'Nope.'

A troubled expression crossed Dad's face and then he nodded, as if he'd made up his mind about something.

'In some ways, Light Magic and Shadow Magic are similar,' he said. 'But only on the surface. To put it simply, Light Magic is good, and using it properly makes you a better person. Shadow Magic gradually takes control of its followers, so gradually that they don't notice until it's too late. In the end, it destroys all their goodness and makes them cruel and cold.'

'But does it come from inside, like Light Magic?'

'Dido,' Dad said severely, 'this is hardly the place to discuss Shadow Magic.'

'OK, OK. No need to get your lingerie in a loop, I was only asking. What does being in harmony with my magic mean exactly?'

'Well, it's – you kind of...' Dad shrugged. 'It's not

something you can put into words, you have to experience it for yourself.'

'How do I do that?'

Dad told Dido to sit cross-legged, took a glass ball down from a shelf and set it on the floor in front of her.

'Do you know what that is?' he said.

'A fortune teller's crystal ball. I thought Mum kept it as a joke.'

'No joke. This is a spirit-mirror, and you have to put a lot of effort into making it work.'

'It doesn't look much like a mirror to me!' snorted Dido. 'Where's the reflection?'

'At the exact centre.'

Dido squinted at the ball.

'How d'you find the exact centre of a thing you can see right through?' she said.

'That's where the effort comes in,' said Dad. 'I'm going back to the house to make a cup of tea. You hang on here for a while, see how far you get.'

Dad bowed to the Goddess and stepped out of the sanctuary.

Dido stared into the crystal. At first she was distracted by noises from outside – the cooing of woodpigeons, the chimes of an ice-cream van – but she slowly managed to shut them out. She could see a distorted version of herself on the surface of the ball, and within, the magnified image of the floorboard beneath it, and she shut them out too.

There was nothing but herself and the clearness of the crystal. At its heart she glimpsed a tiny point of light, drifting like a speck of dust in a shaft of sunlight. She followed the light, drifting with it.

The sanctuary changed. The wooden walls became the trunks of birch trees. The crystal ball formed a pool, fed by a spring that flowed from a pile of dark boulders.

Dido stood up, feeling the springiness of the turf under her feet. She was in a forest clearing. Overhead, the sky was an unbroken blue.

'Where am I?' she said aloud.

'At the centre,' a voice replied.

Someone was standing on the other side of the pool. Dido couldn't tell if the person was a boy or a girl. He, or she, was young and slender, with a shock of almost white curls, almond-shaped eyes that were alarmingly green, and a pointed chin. She, or he, was dressed in grey breeches and a grey, puff-sleeved shirt.

'At the centre of what?' said Dido.

'Your magic.'

'And you would be?'

'Lilil.'

'As in L-I-L-I-L?'

'If you say so,' said Lilil.

Dido thought for a moment.

'That's the same forwards as backwards,' she said.

'Is it?' said Lilil. 'How intriguing.'

'What are you doing here?'

'Talking to you.'

'That's not what I meant.'

'Then you should have asked what you meant, shouldn't you?' Lilil said with a smile. 'If you want the right answers, you have to ask me the right questions.'

Lilil gave Dido a teasing sideways glance. Dido had the uncomfortable feeling that she was being flirted with.

'Are you male or female?' Dido said.

Lilil's eyelashes fluttered. 'Which would you prefer me to be?'

'Let's not go there!' said Dido. 'Let's stay with the right question stuff. What am *I* doing here?'

'You wanted to be inside your magic and you are. I'm the bit of it that can talk to you.'

'So,' said Dido, reasoning it through, 'if my magic

comes from inside me that makes you me, in a way, right?'

'I've been you since the instant you existed,' said Lilil, 'and before that I was someone else.'

'Huh, are you telling me I used to be another person?'

'You can only be you,' Lilil said with a laugh, 'but I've been the witch-spirit of many people over the centuries. Magic isn't like a body that grows old and withers away, it lasts forever. It can be taken from you by a stronger witch, and after your time it will be given to another, but it can never be destroyed.'

'Where did it come from to start with?'

'From what you call the Goddess.'

'Do Shadowmasters have witch-spirits too?' asked Dido.

The playful light in Lilil's eyes went out. 'Of course, but they are not followers of the Goddess. They serve Spelkor, the Lord of Shadow. Some of the spirits once belonged to Light Magic, but Spelkor seduced them with promises of riches and power, and enslaved them to his will.'

'Is that what the Shadowmaster wants – to turn Mum, Dad and me into Spelkor's slaves?' said Dido. 'How can I stop it happening?'

'The Shadowmaster has great strength, Dido,' Lilil said gravely. 'You are not yet ready to do battle with such a formidable enemy.'

This sounded familiar to Dido.

'Don't tell me, let me guess,' she said. 'Next comes a bunch of blah about steering clear of Shadow Magic and sticking to easy things, right?'

'Wrong. The struggle has already begun. That's why I put up the barrier to prevent you from telling your parents what you've learned. They would have forbidden you from doing what needs to be done.'

'Which is?'

'If you wish to survive, you must learn more about your other side. You're the only one who can do this. You must work without your parents' help, and you must work quickly.'

Dido gulped.

'Survival sounds good,' she said. 'What's my other side?'

Lilil walked around the pool and stood beside Dido. 'Look down and tell me the first thing you notice.'

Dido looked down.

'I've got a shadow and you haven't,' she said.

'Good!' said Lilil, sounding pleased. 'I have no

shadow because I'm your Light side, but for every light there is a shadow. You must find your Shadow side and use it.'

'Wouldn't it be quicker to tell me who the Stanstowe Shadowmaster is, so I can zap them before they zap me?'

'Find your Shadow!' Lilil said sternly.

'I don't need to find it,' said Dido. 'It's right there at my feet.'

'Well?' Lilil said.

Dido examined her shadow. It was her dark self. When she moved, it moved. If she ran, it would keep pace with her. She could only lose it in darkness.

'You control it,' said Lilil. 'Set it free.'

Dido looked inside her mind and saw scissors cutting through paper, a mother letting go of a toddler's hand.

The edge of her shadow quivered. It stretched out like a piece of chewy toffee, then separated itself from her feet and flowed across the grass, altering shape and growing fur and paws and ears as it went, until it became a black panther crouching at the pool and drinking, its lapping tongue sending ripples through the water. Muscles moved under its glossy pelt.

'Is that my Shadow side?' Dido said softly.

'Yes.'

'It's beautiful!'

'But deadly,' Lilil said. 'Remember its claws and teeth.'

As if on cue, the panther lifted its head and growled.

'I see what you mean,' said Dido. 'Not too friendly, is it?'

'It will always be wild, Dido, and you'll never tame it, but you can harness its strength to help you take your enemy by surprise. The Shadowmaster will not be expecting you to use Shadow Magic. Only call on it when you have to, and always take care. Shadow Magic is fickle and destructive and can cause harm you did not intend. Use it wisely.'

Lilil, the panther, the pool and the clearing sank back into the sanctuary. There was a loud crack. The crystal ball wobbled. Dido reached out to steady it and noticed that it was no longer perfect. A dark flaw ran through it like a streak of black lightning; Dido's Shadow Magic was already showing her what it could do.

Her feelings weren't so much mixed as scrambled. What Lilil had told her about the Shadowmaster was intriguing and scary, full of hints but not much hard information, which Dido guessed was the way Lilil worked. If only she'd been allowed to stay in her magic longer, she might have been able to come up with some more of the right questions.

At the same time, Dido was proud of herself and thrilled by what she'd achieved. Although she longed to brag to her parents about it, she knew that if she so much as tried, Lilil would stop her with the wall again. Playing it cool was the only way to go.

She picked up the ball and carried it back to the house.

Dad was in the kitchen, drinking tea as he leafed through the Sunday paper.

'Any luck?' he said.

'Kind of, but not lucky luck.'

Dido showed him the ball. Dad turned it over in his hands and tutted.

'Your mother won't be pleased,' he said. 'Don't tell her until I've ordered another one over the Internet. Did you reach your centre?'

'Yeah,' said Dido. 'It's called—'

'Don't tell me! Don't tell anyone. That's your secret name.'

'Have you got a secret name?'

'Everyone has,' said Dad, 'but not everyone can

find it. You're fortunate. The Goddess has granted you a favour.'

Dido thought about the snarling panther, and wondered exactly what kind of favour the Goddess had granted her.

13
The Purple Mirror

At the bus stop, first thing Monday morning, Scott was in a bubbly mood.

'Morning, Dido,' he chirped. 'And what a big, bright, beautiful morning it is!'

Dido, who wasn't awake enough to notice what the morning was like, grimaced. 'What's made you so cheerful?' she said.

'It's Monday.'

'And?'

'Believe me, if you'd spent most of your weekend doing chores, you'd be glad to get back to school too. Plus, I've made a totally amazing discovery.'

'What?'

With a stage conjuror's flourish, Scott produced a piece of string out of thin air. It had been tied into a complicated, lumpy knot with no visible loose ends. 'This is the world's first un-undoable knot!' Scott declared proudly. 'I invented it myself. Brilliant, isn't it? I might take out a patent.'

Dido's frown deepened. Scott's boundless enthusiasm was beginning to irritate her.

'Scott,' she said, 'there's no such thing as an un-undoable knot.'

'There is now.'

'Let me take a look.'

Scott handed over the knot. As soon as Dido closed her fingers around it, her Shadow side took her irritation as an invitation to take over and went into action like a blink of darkness inside her head. She could feel the magic working on the string, making it twist and wriggle, as if a snake were trying to free itself from her grasp.

Dido stopped her Shadow Magic with a holding spell, cobbled together from remembered snapshots of sleeping babies and old cats basking in sunshine. The string went still, but when Dido opened her hand, she saw that the knot had untied itself.

Scott saw it too and his face crumpled.

Dido felt a twinge of guilt.

'Sorry, Scott,' she said. 'I didn't mean to—'

'How did you do that?'

'Magic. I'm a witch, remember?'

'That joke is so past its sell-by date.'

'It was an accident,' said Dido.

But she was fibbing. Untying the knot hadn't been an accident at all. She'd never used her magic to do anything mean before, and was ashamed of herself.

'Can't you retie it?' she said.

'What's the point of retying an un-undoable knot that's undoable?' said Scott. 'It took me ages. I was positive I'd cracked it.' He sounded miserable.

Dido thought, It's only a dumb knot, for goodness' sake, then pulled herself up short. Hey, wait a minute, that's no excuse! You spoiled something that was important to someone you're supposed to be friends with, Dido.

She was going to have to keep a wary eye on her Shadow side; it could evidently creep up and take her unawares. To take the edge off her guilt, she told Scott about making friends with Philippa on Saturday, tactfully editing out Philippa's family problems. It worked too, because when she'd finished, Scott said, 'Does that make her my friend too? Cool!'

Dido's resolve to keep her Shadow side in check received a severe testing at school. As soon as she and

Scott walked through the main gate, a voice called out, 'Look who it isn't! The new Deputy Head's kid.'

Jack, Ross and David were lounging against the wall of the boiler house.

'What was that?' said Dido.

'Know what your Mum's nickname is?' Jack said. 'Mrs Nosebit. She's called that 'cos she's so snotty. Got any bits up your nose, Dido?'

Ross and David tittered.

Anger came on stealthy paws, the tips of its canine teeth showing white against its black muzzle. Power surged through Dido. She could hurt The Terrible Trio, force them down on to all fours, begging her to stop. They'd be too afraid to ever make fun of her again.

Dido's thumbs suddenly itched so sharply that they stung. The pain distracted her long enough for her inseeing eye to show that Jack still had the mischief spell around his neck. If she'd given in to the temptation to use magic on him, she might have found herself back at the circle.

Dido thought, When Lilil said my Shadow side could do harm without my intending it to, she forgot to mention that includes hurting myself.

'What's going on here?' a voice called.

It was Mr Purdey, on playground patrol before the start of school. As he walked over, his presence drained all the swagger out of The Terrible Trio and reduced them to what they actually were, three kids caught name-calling.

'What are you boys up to?' Mr Purdey demanded.

'Nothing, Sir,' said Jack, squirming. 'We were just talking.'

Mr Purdey turned to Dido.

'Is that so?' he asked.

'Yes, Sir,' said Dido. 'Jack asked me about my weekend.'

'Come with me a moment, will you, Dido?'

Dido followed Mr Purdey to the side of the main gate. Mr Purdey turned his back to Scott and The Terrible Trio so that they wouldn't be able to hear him.

'Are you sure those boys weren't making fun of you?' he said.

'No, Sir,' said Dido. 'I mean, yes I'm sure that they weren't making fun.'

'Well, if they were, you should tell me now. Bullying of that kind has a habit of getting out of hand.'

'I know, Sir. I've been to school before.'

Mr Purdey nodded. 'All right, but remember I'm there if you need me,' he said, and left her to continue his patrol.

By the time Dido rejoined Scott, The Terrible Trio had already slunk off.

'What did Mr Purdey want?' said Scott.

'To ask me if Jack and his gang were bullying me. I told him they weren't.'

'Why didn't you drop them in it? They deserved it.'

'I fight my own battles, thanks,' Dido said tartly; then she softened her tone and said, 'I suppose you won't want to be mates with me now you know about my mum.'

'Don't talk soft! I've known about your mum since day one. You can't help who your parents are, can you? Anyway, I like Mrs Nesbit. She's funky.'

'Funky?'

'For a Deputy Head,' said Scott.

Dido couldn't work out if this was a good thing or not.

Philippa was waiting on her own outside C Block. When she saw Dido and Scott approaching, she went to greet them.

'Hi, Philippa,' said Dido. 'You know Scott, don't you?'

Scott said, 'Hi, Philippa. Ever tied anybody up?'

Philippa's face registered shock.

'Have I *what?*' she squeaked.

Dido laughed.

'Don't mind Scott,' she said. 'He fancies a career as an escape artist.'

'Really?' said Philippa. 'That's, um, an unusual ambition.'

'Interesting too,' Scott said. 'For instance...'

There were enough for-instances to last until registration.

Philippa changed places and sat with Dido and Scott in the form room, which didn't go unnoticed. Dido found herself on the wrong end of some looks from Mandy and Charlotte, and guessed that they'd classified her as a loser, as well as Philippa. Having friends was proving to be as tricky as having a Shadow side.

The morning went smoothly. Philippa and Scott seemed to hit it off: Philippa laughed at Scott's jokes and Scott enjoyed cracking them, because it gave him an excuse to look at her. The Terrible

Trio left them alone; the unpleasantly close encounter with Mr Purdey had obviously put the frighteners on them. In fact, things went so smoothly that Dido was temporarily able to forget that she was a witch.

Years before in the Juniors, during a Science lesson that had ended in a flood, Dido had discovered that school and magic didn't mix. Mum had explained to her at great length that it would be disrespectful to insee her teachers, and that getting hold of test papers in advance by making them fly into her room at midnight was cheating. So keeping her magic under wraps in the classroom was automatic; besides, she might get caught, and then there'd be a lot of awkward explaining to do.

At lunchtime, Dido and Philippa headed for the girls' loos, and ran into Ollie on their way.

'Hey, Dido,' Ollie said. 'I was hoping we'd meet up today. I had this well-weird dream about you on Saturday night.'

'You did?' said Dido, not knowing what to expect.

'Yeah. You were on the top of Stanstowe Hill, you know, near that stone circle? And you were glowing.'

'Glowing?'

'You had this white light all around you. You looked awesome.'

'Must've been the sun,' said Dido. 'Didn't you know? It shines out of my butt.'

Ollie and Philippa laughed; Dido joined in, but only to hide her concern. She suspected that Ollie had picked up something from her on Saturday afternoon. Some people were naturally sensitive to magic – in folk tales this was called second sight. It came in various forms. Some people had visions of the future, others dreamed dreams that came true, but everyone who had second sight could detect the presence of magic. If Ollie could, he might guess that Dido was a witch. Rather than risk being found out, Dido was going to have to keep Ollie at a distance, which was a shame because she liked him. She considered inseeing Ollie to check him out, but then thought that he might be aware of it. She remembered one of her Dad's sayings about when to use magic and when not to use it – when in doubt, don't!

'How's that brother of yours?' Philippa asked Ollie.

Ollie's reply was lengthy and involved, and Dido left them to it; her need for the loo was threatening to reach critical level.

The loos were empty when Dido stepped out of the cubicle. She went to the washbasins, and while she was soaping her hands, she glanced in the eye-level mirror.

She didn't see herself in it.

The mirror was filled with purple smoke that seethed and rolled; the edges of the mirror wobbled, as though the wall behind it had turned to jelly.

Dido quickly recovered from her initial surprise and swallowed a fit of nervous laughter. The mirror looked ridiculous, like a tacky special effect in a made-for-TV movie.

Dido heard a voice in her head. It sounded neither male nor female, but so old that Dido thought of cobwebbed crypts with slimy walls. She shuddered as she realised that it was the voice of the Shadowmaster.

'I know you, Light Witch.'

'And I know you,' said Dido, determined not to show how alarmed she felt. 'Am I supposed to be scared? Is this the best you can do, Shadowmaster?'

The sinister voice sent ice down Dido's spine; the soundtrack was a lot scarier than the visuals.

'You know nothing, child, but you can learn.

Come to me. I will teach you to walk in the paths of Shadow, and all that you desire shall be yours.'

The smoke in the mirror cleared. Dido saw herself walking on stage to address an International Light Witch Conference. Light Witches from all over the world were rising to their feet and applauding, while flashguns went off like strobe lights.

'Surrender to me. Shadow is good. Shadow is great.'

Now the mirror showed a table piled with books. The topmost book had its title tooled into the leather of the cover. It was *The Chronicles of Astarte*, a legendary long-lost work that was supposed to contain the secrets of all magic, Light and Shadow.

'Surrender. Surrender...'

The door of the loos banged open and Philippa appeared, breaking the spell.

The mirror returned to its usual self.

Dido hummed a shielding charm – drawn curtains, locked chests and suits of armour – and went on washing her hands.

'You sound happy,' Philippa remarked.

'Why shouldn't I be happy?' said Dido. 'Everything's just dandy.'

But it wasn't. The identity of the Shadowmaster remained a mystery, but the Shadowmaster knew who she was and where to find her. The danger was getting bigger and closer with each passing minute.

14
A Show of Strength

The following morning, when Mum put out the kitchen rubbish, she found the crystal ball. She took it into the dining room and plonked it down on the table in front of Dad and Dido.

'What's this doing in the bin?' she asked.

The crystal ball was covered with coffee grounds and bits of eggshell, and looked sad.

Dido and Dad said, 'E-e-r.'

'Well?' said Mum. 'I'm waiting for an explanation.'

'It was an accident,' Dido said. 'I was searching for my centre and the ball broke.'

Mum was furious.

'How could you be so careless, Dido?' she barked. 'I've told you time and time again not to meddle with things that you're not ready for.'

'It's my fault,' said Dad. 'I told Dido about the spirit-mirror and how to use it. A replacement's on its way. We didn't tell you about it because we didn't want to upset you.'

'Honestly, you two are as irresponsible as each other,' Mum said. 'I leave you alone for five minutes and you ruin a family heirloom.'

'My family heirloom,' Dad pointed out. 'It belonged to my grandmother.'

'That's not the point, Peter.' It was never a good sign when Mum called Dad *Peter*. 'You tried to hide the cracked ball from me. Why? Have I suddenly turned into an ogre who bites heads off whenever something goes wrong?'

Dad and Dido didn't say anything.

Mum's anger went from hot to cold.

'So that's it,' she said quietly. 'I can't be trusted any longer. I have to have things kept from me because I can't cope with the strain of my new job. What else don't I know about?'

'Faye,' said Dad, 'don't you think you're being a tad unreasonable?'

Mum promptly turned on her heel and stormed out. She gave the front door a slam that made the entire house shake.

'Well, that went well,' said Dad. 'The problem is, your mother's right. She's not coping with the new job. I've never known her to be this stressed about teaching before, and she's turning into a workaholic.'

Or maybe the Shadowmaster is putting pressure on Mum to disrupt my home life, Dido thought, getting at me through the people I care about, hoping I'll get mad enough to lash out and make a mistake.

Reading fairy tales had taught Dido that Shadowmasters didn't just go in for spectacular spells. Being petty-minded and nasty could be just as effective. In the original Brothers Grimm version of *Cinderella*, the Ugly Sisters cut off their toes and heels to make their feet fit the glass slipper – a classic example of Shadow Magic in action, persuading people to harm themselves in the hope of getting something that they wanted, and then taking it away from them afterwards.

'D'you think you could talk to your mother at school today, Dido?' said Dad. 'You know, do a bit of grovelling and say how sorry we are? It would come better from you than from me. Appeal to her maternal instinct.'

'And what will you do?'

'I feel a cliché coming on, one with a bottle of champagne and a bunch of red roses in it.'

'You'd better buy thornless roses, just in case,' Dido advised.

After registration, Seven North scampered across the campus, eager for their second Drama lesson. There was a buzz of excited chatter in the corridor outside the Drama studio, but when Miss Morgan opened the door and held up her hand, the silence was instant.

'Go in, put your bags down and form a circle,' Miss Morgan said.

The class did as they were told. Miss Morgan went to stand in the middle of the circle.

'I'm going to hum a note and I want you to join in when I point to you,' she said. 'If I raise my right hand, hum louder. If I raise my left hand, hum softly.'

The note started simply, then blossomed as voices were added to it. Two people were tone deaf and joined in off-key, producing a weird harmony. The note held the class together, and made them a part of something that Miss Morgan controlled; it swelled into a crescendo, then slowly died away.

'That sound has given you magic,' said Miss Morgan. 'You have power over people. Whatever move you make, they have to move in the same way, like a reflection in a mirror. In groups of two or three, choose a leader and explore your magic...now!'

The class divided up; Dido, Scott and Philippa worked together.

'Who's going to be leader?' Dido said.

'You,' said Scott. 'You're already magic because you're a witch.'

'What?' gasped Philippa.

'Private joke,' Scott told her. 'Dido's a witch and I'm Voodini, master of escapes.'

Philippa laughed, thinking that Scott was kidding. Scott joined in the laugh because he thought he was kidding too.

Dido kept it easy at first, taking a step towards Scott and Philippa, then a step back. Gradually she added other movements, swinging her arms, changing direction without warning. Scott and Philippa followed, so that the three of them moved as one.

'Good!' said Miss Morgan. 'Now change leaders.'

'Your turn, Philippa,' Dido said.

The air around Philippa crackled and tiny blue sparks swarmed in her hair. Her eyes rolled up until the whites showed. She shuddered, every muscle in her body twitching violently.

'What the—?' whispered Scott.

Philippa stood on tiptoe and rose several centimetres off the floor, floating on nothing. She teetered from side to side, like a top beginning to lose momentum.

'Er, Dido?' said Scott. 'What's Philippa doing?'

Dido didn't hear him, because all her attention was on Miss Morgan.

Miss Morgan was gazing straight at Philippa. She didn't look surprised or shocked that Philippa was suspended in mid-air.

Dido's inseeing took over and turned her towards Philippa.

The Shadowmaster had obviously decided that it was time for a show of strength. The spell had taken the form of a harpy – an eagle with a woman's head. Instead of hair, the woman's face was surrounded by a twisting mass of serpents that hissed, and flicked out their forked tongues. The harpy's bronze talons were sunk into Philippa's shoulders and its wings quivered as it hovered, holding Philippa in the air.

Nothing Dido had learned in Light Magic had prepared her for anything like this, but her Shadow Magic knew what had to be done, and it contemptuously ignored Dido's no-magic-in-the-classroom rule. It shot out a glittering net of red light that wrapped itself around the harpy. The creature shrieked and struggled, but the net tightened mercilessly, cutting through feathers and flesh. The talons loosed their grip; Philippa came down with a bump and a scream; the harpy and the net winked into nothingness.

Seven North had been so engrossed in the lesson that no one noticed what had happened to Philippa, but when she screamed the entire class stopped what it was doing and stared at her.

'What's the matter, Philippa?' Miss Morgan asked.

Philippa sobbed hysterically. Dido couldn't think what to say because she was too startled. Miss Morgan *knew* what was the matter with Philippa – she'd seen it with her own eyes – so why was she pretending that she hadn't?

It was Scott who came to the rescue.

'A big spider ran across the floor, Miss,' he said, improvising. 'Philippa's afraid of spiders. It gave her a shock.'

'Take her outside and calm her down,' said Miss Morgan. 'The rest of you, carry on.'

In the corridor, Philippa sagged against Dido.

'What was it, Dido?' Philippa wailed. 'What happened to me?'

'Steady,' said Dido. 'It's OK. You're safe.'

Scott looked at Dido, his face pale.

'Was that magic?' he said.

'Yes,' said Dido.

'You weren't kidding, were you?'

'No.'

Scott's eyes bulged in shock. 'You r-really are a—'

'Like I told you,' said Dido. 'Don't you dare blab it around.'

'Or you'll turn me into a frog, right?'

'I can't turn people into frogs,' said Dido. 'I haven't got to that part yet.'

Philippa was still so jittery at the end of the lesson that Miss Morgan told her to go home, but she asked Dido to stay behind.

An eerie silence fell over the Drama studio, and the darkness in the gloomy corners seemed to deepen.

Miss Morgan said, 'Be careful, Dido.'

'Careful of what, Miss?' said Dido, playing the innocent.

'Sometimes when you play a trick on someone, it can come back on you.'

'I didn't play any tricks, Miss.'

'It would be very wrong of you to take advantage

of your special situation, don't you think?'

Dido was alarmed.

'What special situation would that be, Miss?' she said.

'Having your mother as one of the Deputy Heads of this school, of course,' Miss Morgan said with a smile. 'Some teachers might be nervous about disciplining you because your mother is a senior member of staff, but I'm not one of them. Remember that in future. You'd better go now, or you'll be late for your next lesson.'

Dido left the Drama studio, feeling decidedly uneasy. Perhaps breaking the spell on Philippa had tired her to the point of paranoia, or perhaps Miss Morgan had sussed more about Dido than Dido would have liked, but she was certain that Miss Morgan had seen Philippa floating in the air, and Miss Morgan hadn't mentioned a thing about it.

Why not? thought Dido. Is she used to that kind of thing?

And with that thought, came other thoughts that Dido didn't find at all welcome.

Miss Morgan had charmed Seven North in a way that didn't seem normal, and Philippa had been enchanted by Shadow Magic in the middle of Miss Morgan's lesson.

Was Miss Morgan the Stanstowe Shadowmaster?

Scott didn't say much for the rest of the morning, but Dido could feel him thinking and wished that she knew what was going through his mind. She considered using inseeing on him, but she was afraid of what she might find out, and anyway, it was a mates thing, not a magic thing.

Scott opened up during the lunch break. After eating in the cafeteria, he and Dido took a stroll around the edge of the playing fields, where they could talk without being overheard.

Scott said, 'Why did you make Philippa float around like that, Dido? Don't you like her?'

'It wasn't me,' said Dido. 'I didn't cast a spell on her. I broke one.'

'But if it wasn't you...' Scott gulped. 'Are you telling me there's *another* witch around here?'

'Stanstowe's very own Shadowmaster.'

'Huh?'

Dido squeezed centuries of tradition into a single sentence.

'Shadowmasters are the bad guys,' she said.

'And you're not…?'

'I'm a Light Witch.'

'Why would the Shadowmaster pick on Philippa?'

'To get at me,' said Dido, guessing. 'To show me that he – or she – can get at my friends.'

'Who's the Shadowmaster?'

'Your guess is as good as mine. I'm working on it.'

'What will you do when you find out?'

'I'm working on that too.'

'Can't you conjure up a demon who'll tell you?'

'Forget the Disney stuff, Scott,' Dido said. 'Magic isn't like that.'

'Then what is it like?'

'Hard to explain and best left to the experts.'

'Fair enough.' Scott leaned closer to Dido. 'How about a quick demonstration?'

'Absolutely not! I don't do tricks to entertain people. Being a witch is a serious business.'

'Don't you have any fun at all?'

'It's a big responsibility.'

'Oh. So you couldn't use your magical skills to pass SATs or anything?'

'I could, but I wouldn't. D'you mind?'

'What?'

'That I'm a witch.'

'Nah!' said Scott. 'Having a witch as a mate is kind of cool.'

After last lesson, Dido went to talk to her mother. She was dreading having to apologise about the crystal ball; given the mood Mum had been in lately, she was liable to go ballistic.

Cautiously Dido approached the door labelled Deputy Head, and just as she was about to knock, she spotted something that made her hesitate.

There were faint marks on the paintwork of the door that were only visible when the light caught them at a right angle. The scratches formed a pentagram, like the sign for The Pentacle, and in each of its points was a symbol. Dido recognised some of them from old books of magic: they were curse marks called hexes, and they brought their victims bad luck.

No wonder Mum's been bad-tempered! Dido thought.

The evidence against Miss Morgan seemed to be piling up. The bewitched grey cat could be her familiar. She could easily have been the one who'd put the spells on Jack and Philippa, and the mirror in the girls' loos, and she would have had access to Mum's door to draw the pentagon.

The problem was, how was Dido going to explain it all to Mum?

15
Second Sight

The pentagram shimmered like gossamer and was elegant in its way, but Dido had no desire to see what had spun it. She put together a spell that contained dusters, kitchen towels and blotting paper, and erased the pentagram with it. The Shadowmaster hadn't gone to any great lengths to hex Mum, just enough to keep her stressed and crabby. It was a risky thing to do, because under normal circumstances, Mum would have been able to detect the hex. But Mum wouldn't have expected a pentacle on her door at school any more than Dido had. It gave a tiny clue as to what was going on in the Shadowmaster's mind. If it *was* Miss Morgan, she was confident, maybe overconfident, and knowing that might give Dido an advantage at some point.

Dido knocked at the door and waited for Mum to say, 'Come in.'

Mum was at her desk, working her way through a thick wad of papers. Her reading glasses were balanced on the tip of her nose and she peered over them.

'Can't this wait, Dido?' she said. 'I'm up to my eyeballs at the moment. I've had a thumping headache all day and—' Mum broke off and raised her eyebrows. 'Oh, it's gone now. That's something to be thankful for at least.'

'It must be the effect of seeing me,' Dido said airily. 'I came to say that I'm really, really sorry about the crystal ball and that Dad and I didn't tell you.'

'Accidents happen,' said Mum, shrugging dismissively. 'I know you didn't mean to do it. I'd rather the crystal ball was damaged than you.'

Mum sounded so much like her old self that Dido chanced pushing her luck.

'Mum, can you call Dad and tell him I'll be late home? I want to go round to Philippa's house and see if she's OK.'

'What's wrong with Philippa?'

Dido hesitated, weighing up how much to tell Mum. If she told her the whole truth, she could just imagine what Mum's reaction would be: 'And how did you come to know how to break a Shadow Magic spell, Dido?' Which would lead to more questions, and Dido getting herself deeper and deeper into trouble. Besides, Lilil had put up a barrier to stop Dido telling her parents what she'd learned about Shadow Magic before. What would stop Lilil doing the same now? Dido decided to play safe by being vague.

'She nearly had an accident in Drama this morning, but I managed to save her,' she said.

'Well done, you!'

Dido counted to three and added, 'By using magic.'

Mum sat bolt upright in her chair.

'What magic?' she said.

'A shielding spell.'

'Dido!' Mum groaned. 'How many times have I told you—?'

'I know, I know. But it was an emergency and I didn't have a choice. If you'd been there you would have done the same thing. Only...'

'There's more?' said Mum.

'Philippa was badly upset and Miss Morgan sent her home. Miss Morgan talked to me at the end of the lesson, and I had this funny feeling.'

'What sort of a funny feeling?'

'That she'd twigged about my magic.'

Mum shut her eyes, shook her head and sighed wearily.

'This is exactly the kind of mess you get into if you use your magic at school,' she said. 'That's why your father and I keep nagging you to keep it secret.' The thought that occurred to Mum made her eyes spring open. 'You didn't insee Alice Morgan, did you?'

'Of course not! I may act dumb sometimes, but I'm not *that* dumb.'

'Thank goodness for that!' said Mum. 'Leave Alice Morgan to me. I'll find out how much she knows.'

'How will you do that?'

'Inseeing.'

'Oh, so I'm not allowed to insee my teachers, but it's cool for you to do it? That's fair,' Dido said sarcastically.

'There's a difference,' Mum said. 'You're still learning, and you tend to charge into things. With my experience, I can use the subtle approach. In the meantime, no magic at school, right?'

'Hmm.'

'Will you put a forgetting spell on Philippa?'

'No. If she knows what happened, I'll talk her out of believing it. Even inexperienced witches like me can be subtle when they have to.'

Dido set off for Philippa's house. She knew that Philippa's street wasn't far from Prince Arthur's, but she didn't know precisely where it was, or the house's number. She was depending on her trusty thumbs to produce the goods.

It was amazing how quickly the school emptied at the end of the day. Fifteen-hundred pupils had vanished without trace, and the campus was almost deserted – almost, but not quite.

The silver tabby was under the arch of the main gate, cleaning itself. It licked a paw and rubbed its whiskers, so intent on what it was doing that it failed to register that Dido was there.

Dido's mind raced. She had a strong hunch that the tabby belonged to the Shadowmaster, and if she could catch the cat she might be able to discover who its owner was.

Stay put, puss! she thought. If I can get a couple of metres closer to you...

She pictured a bucket filled with wallpaper paste, and a tube of superglue, and her Light Magic cast a spell that stiffened the cat into a statue.

Dido hurried forwards. The spell protecting the cat resisted her magic with a grating sound that set Dido's teeth on edge. Before she could reach the archway, her spell broke and the cat bolted into a clump of rose bushes on the lawn outside the school entrance.

Dido hunkered down and scrabbled around, but all she could find were three silver hairs caught on a thorn.

Better than nothing, she thought, removing them from the bush and slipping them into the top pocket of her shirt. Shame I couldn't—

'Really, Dido! I would have thought better of you.'

Dido stood up and found herself face to face with Dr Parker. His hypnotic brown eyes held her gaze.

'I was only—' Dido blurted.

'Teasing a helpless animal like that. I thought you liked cats.'

'I do, Sir, but...' Dido's voice stuck in her throat. A massive blush burned her face.

'I have to confess that I'm rather disappointed,' said Dr Parker. 'I took you for a gentle person.'

Dido's blush deepened. Dr Parker had a strange ability to make her feel guilty, despite the fact that she wasn't. His charisma was like a force field.

'I wanted to see whether it had a collar on, or whether it was a stray,' Dido said feebly.

'I'll give you the benefit of the doubt this once,' said Dr Parker. 'I expect a high standard of behaviour from you, Dido. Bear that in mind, and don't let me catch you doing anything like this again.'

'No, Sir. Thank you, Sir.'

After she'd taken five paces, Dido thought, Wait up, I said *thank you*. What was I thanking the guy for?

For releasing her from his presence, she decided. Dr Parker had an inner strength that went far beyond his role as an authority figure. He could see deep inside people; it was a rare ability, and one that left Dido puzzled as to how he'd come by it.

Had she got Miss Morgan all wrong? Perhaps Dr Parker was the Shadowmaster.

Dido's thumbs led her to Number 49 Hazelwood Close. She rang the bell, and the door was opened by a young boy with a shock of mousy hair. He had a snub nose, freckles, and looked cute.

'Does Philippa Trevelyan live here?' said Dido.

The boy scowled.

''Fraid so,' he said.

'You must be Tom, yeah?'

'Uh-huh.'

'I'm Dido.'

'Hurrah for you,' said Tom.

Dido grinned at Tom's cheek; it reminded her of her own.

'Is Philippa feeling better?' she said.

'See for yourself, she's in the lounge. She's popular today – can't understand it myself.'

Tom's comment about Philippa's popularity became clear when Dido entered the lounge. Philippa was in an armchair in the bay window, and seated on a sofa to her right was Ollie.

'Dido!' said Philippa. 'You should have rung ahead and let me know, we could've had a party.'

'I won't stay long,' said Dido. 'I just wanted to check on how you were.'

'Same here!' said Ollie, a shade too quickly. 'The goss said Philippa had gone home ill, so, as her house is on my way home, and I was passing, I thought I'd pop in and, um...'

'I'm fine,' said Philippa, 'except for feeling dead stupid about freaking over a spider. Still, it was pretty humungous – talk about tarantulas!'

Philippa was doing what people did when they were faced with the inexplicable: she'd seized on what Scott had said and convinced herself that there had actually been a spider in the Drama studio. If she remembered anything about floating off the ground, she wasn't letting on.

Dido ticked a worry off her list and said, 'Yeah, it was spectacular, wasn't it? I nearly screamed too.'

Philippa, Dido and Ollie chatted about this, that and nothing in particular. It was standard Year Seven stuff, but Dido sensed a tension in the room, as if she'd interrupted something between Philippa and Ollie. She wondered if Ollie had been about to ask Philippa out, and it made her feel that she was in the way.

Thinking that she'd better do the decent thing and make a strategic withdrawal, Dido said, 'Is that the time? I must be off.'

'I'll come with you,' said Ollie. 'Take it easy, Philippa.'

Philippa looked crestfallen. 'Can't you both hang around for a while?' she said. 'My dad won't be home for half an hour. You can help me babysit Tom.'

'Sorry,' said Ollie. 'Urgent appointment with Maths homework.'

'English,' said Dido. 'Will you be back at school tomorrow, Philippa?'

'I guess,' Philippa said. 'If you meet any big spiders on your way home, squish them for me, will you?'

Outside on the street, Dido couldn't keep her mouth in check and started to babble.

'It must be a bummer to have arachnophobia that badly. I mean, I'm not fond of spiders, but Philippa was, like, paralysed with fear. I've never seen anyone so scared. Hang on, though, yes I have. There was this girl in my junior school who had a thing about moths. One day in assembly—'

'I know, Dido,' said Ollie.

'Huh?'

'I know you're magical.'

Dido was stunned, but tried to bluff her way out.

'Really?' she said, patting her hair. 'What does it for you – my eyes or my irresistible personality?'

'Stop pretending, Dido. You're a witch, aren't you? You've got that thing my gran had.'

'What thing?'

Ollie screwed up his eyes and squinted at Dido.

'An aura,' he said. 'It's like you're wrapped in the Northern Lights. I used to see the same thing around my gran, and she was a witch, so you must be too.'

Dido dropped her act because it was pointless. Her suspicions about Ollie were true.

'You've got second sight,' she said.

'Second sight, sixth sense, whatever. I'd rather have had the full magic Monty and been a witch myself, but there you go.'

'Who have you told about me?'

'No one. Why would I?'

'Because most people—'

'I'm not most people,' said Ollie.

Dido was confused and dismayed. This was different to telling Scott she was a witch, because she knew Scott was trustworthy, and telling him had been a way of cementing their friendship. But Ollie had power. Her big secret was out and she felt exposed. The thing that she'd always feared most – that someone would discover the truth about her – was right there, staring out of Ollie's eyes.

Her feeling of panic must have showed on her face, because Ollie said, 'Relax, Dido. I'm on your side. I think you might need my help – or do I need yours? Somebody needs somebody's help anyway.'

Dido thought that she knew what was coming and said, 'There's something wrong at school, isn't there?'

'It's not just school, it's Stanstowe,' said Ollie. 'The whole town is cursed.'

16
Allies

Ollie walked Dido to the bus stop, giving her a potted version of his life story along the way.

'When I was a toddler, Mum and Dad worked during the day, so they left me with Gran,' he said. 'She more or less brought me up. When I could talk, she taught me all these songs and poems. At the time I thought they were nursery rhymes, but now I realise that they were spells.'

'Did you ever try any of them out?' said Dido.

'Yeah, but zilch happened. I think Gran was disappointed that she didn't pass her magic on to me, but I picked up bits and pieces from keeping my ears open. Gran had a reputation for being a faith healer, you know, the laying on of hands and stuff? But she also told fortunes and gave advice on people's love lives. There was always someone dropping by to ask her for help.'

'Did she know you had second sight?'

Ollie nodded.

'She told me she knew from the first time she held me, when I was a new-born baby,' he said. 'The gift, she called it. If I asked her who gave me the gift, all she said was the Goddess, but she'd never say which goddess, like it was bad luck to name her. Weird, eh?'

'Er...not really,' said Dido.

'Gran trained me to use the gift, explained how it worked, what I could and couldn't do with it. By then I'd sussed what she was, but I didn't think there was anything peculiar about it. Gran was Gran, this warm, loving person. She didn't fly around on a broomstick, or live in a gingerbread house. She didn't do anyone any harm – just the opposite. So when I saw your aura, it didn't faze me. As a matter of fact, it was a big relief.'

'How come?' said Dido.

'You're the first witch I've sensed since Gran died. I thought I'd never meet one again, until you showed up. Believe me, Stanstowe could use a friendly witch right now. The curse is getting stronger.'

They reached the bus stop. Ollie flipped down one of the hinged seats for Dido, and the seat next to it for himself.

'Tell me more about the curse,' Dido said.

Ollie smoothed back a lock of hair that had fallen across his forehead.

'It took me years to recognise that it was there,' he said. 'I grew up with it around me, so it was part of what I thought was normal. Then, one summer, my parents took Steve and me on a fortnight's holiday in Cornwall. That was the longest I'd ever been away from home, and when we got back, I noticed how different Stanstowe was to the other towns we'd visited.'

'In what way?'

Ollie's face crinkled as he searched for the right words.

'I see it as a thick fog,' he said, 'and it's this really yucky shade of—'

'Purple?' said Dido, remembering the mirror in the girls' loos.

'You've seen it too?'

'Something like it. What does the fog do?'

'People lose themselves in it. It gets inside their heads and messes them up. Every town has problems – crime, kids on alcohol and drugs – but Stanstowe has its fair share and then some. Once you've noticed the curse it's obvious, but people don't seem to notice. You can't open the local paper without reading a story about teenage suicide, or tramps getting beaten up, or drunken yobbos vandalising the town centre. It goes right down to little things – like did you know that Stanstowe holds the UK record for growing deformed vegetables?'

'What?' said Dido.

'You know, vegetables shaped like Winston Churchill, or people's naughty bits? They run a special photo feature in the paper, Rude Roots. I used to think it was hilarious until I realised it was part of the curse. I tell you, if Stanstowe was a person, a psychiatrist would say that it was headed for a nervous breakdown.'

'I knew it!' said Dido. 'The first time I came here, I knew that something wasn't right. Who laid the curse?'

'Search me, but I know where it comes from – the Speaking Stones on Stanstowe Hill. Have you been up there?'

'Yes, and it's Creeps Central.'

'That's where the curse lives,' said Ollie. 'Hey, is that your bus that just came around the corner?'

Dido looked and said, 'Uh-huh.'

'Great! And there I was just starting to enjoy

myself. You have no idea how brilliant it is to be able to talk to someone about this stuff instead of keeping it to myself.'

'Oh, yes I do,' said Dido.

She meant it: all her life, she'd been isolated by the secret of her magic; the only people she'd been able to discuss it with were her parents, and even then she hadn't been able to discuss everything, like Shadow Magic, for instance. Now Dido had someone who understood, someone she could trust and confide in, plus he was aware of things that she wasn't aware of – like the curse – which might come in handy. Her magic had found her an ally, and it felt terrific.

'We should talk about all this again some time,' said Ollie.

'No question,' Dido said, 'and the sooner the better.'

On the bus ride home, Dido was in an optimistic mood. She had two leads on the Shadowmaster – the stone circle and the hairs from the silver tabby. Dido wasn't absolutely clear about how to follow up the leads; she needed to pump someone's brains, and she knew just the person…

*

Things couldn't have worked out more neatly if Dido had arranged them with a spell. When she arrived home, Dad was mowing the last section of the back lawn. Cosmo was stretched out on the patio, purring like mad because she loved watching humans work themselves into a sweat.

Dido helped Dad with the lawnmower, winding in the flex while he cleaned grass off the blades with a wire brush.

'How's your friend?' asked Dad.

'Better.'

'Your mother sounded better too. Whatever you said to her seems to have worked. Did you have to get down on your hands and knees?'

'Not quite,' said Dido.

As if on cue, Cosmo sauntered past to investigate the garage. The garage was packed with gardening tools, bags of compost, boxes of old magazines and books that hadn't been sorted out during the move and that would probably never be, plus various jars, jugs and ornaments. About the only thing that wasn't in the garage was a car; there was no room for one.

'Dad,' Dido said, 'why do witches have cats as pets?'

'They're not pets, they're familiars,' Dad corrected

her. 'They're partners in magic and they don't have to be cats. Cats are traditional, but I once knew a witch who had a pig as her familiar.'

'What are familiars for?'

'A lot of things. Animals are more instinctive than we are, and their senses are sharper. They're aware of things that are beyond us. Familiars are guardians and guides, and they can't talk, so they're excellent at keeping secrets.'

'Cosmo talks.'

'Yes, but not in a language that we can understand.'

Dido thought, Speak for yourself, I can understand her just fine.

'Familiars are important to witches,' Dad went on. 'They share a part of the spirits of their owners. That's why we put protection spells on them. In the wrong hands, a familiar could be used as a weapon.'

'Which part of whose spirit does Cosmo share – yours, Mum's or mine?'

'A little of us all, I suppose,' said Dad.

Dido supposed not; Cosmo was definitely her cat, despite what Dad believed.

So, thought Dido, the silver cat shares part of the Shadowmaster's spirit.

It was an interesting discovery, but seemed to be a dead end. Dido hadn't learned any spells that would allow her to use the cat hairs to find the Shadowmaster, and if she asked Dad to teach her one, she'd have to field a lot of tricky questions about why she wanted to know. It was time to explore the second lead and find out more about the Speaking Stones.

'Is it OK for me to borrow your laptop to get online?' Dido said. 'I have to look something up for a project.'

She was careful not to mention *which* project.

'All right,' said Dad. 'The laptop's in the lounge, but be careful with it. Don't drop it, don't delete any files and don't forget to plug in the modem. The phone socket's—'

'I know, I know! You can be a real nag sometimes, can't you?'

'It's what fathers are for,' Dad said.

In the lounge, Dido set up the laptop and typed in Stanstowe. The results page gave her a list of sites for a town of the same name in America. Dido tried again with Stanstowe, UK, and was presented with the details of Stanstowe's hotels and guest houses.

'Come on!' Dido said to the computer. 'This is

supposed to be the Information Age, so make with the information!'

Dido's third try was Stanstowe, Local History and it turned out to be lucky. She clicked on the site at the top of the page, and a menu opened.

Stanstowe Local History

We update this site constantly with entries by local contributors. If you know any interesting facts about Stanstowe's history, e-mail them to us at *www.localhistory.stanstowe.co.uk*

I could e-mail you some facts that would make your hair curl, Dido thought grimly.

On the left-hand side of the menu was an index, and under the heading, Sites of Archaeological Interest, Dido saw The Speaking Stones. When she touched the entry with the cursor, the letters stood out in bold type.

Dido double-clicked.

The monitor screen went black, then a purple mist began to appear. Dido could feel cold waves coming off the screen, and it felt like sitting in front of the open door of a fridge. Deep inside the mist, bright dots spelled out a message...

You didn't think it was going to be that easy, did you, Light Witch?

There was a sound like an underground train approaching a station, a rushing roar that grew louder and louder.

Dido hit the Control and Quit buttons; the monitor screen chimed and went dead.

The Shadowmaster had been one step ahead of her. Dido felt frustrated at being out-thought and outmanoeuvred, and a little frightened because the Shadowmaster seemed to be everywhere.

I'm getting hacked off with this, she thought. Trust me to wind up with a Shadowmaster who's computer-literate.

Cosmo curled around the lounge door. She saw the computer on Dido's lap, twisted her top lip back in a snarl and made a chattering noise.

'Yeah, you're right,' Dido admitted. 'What with TV and computers, human beings spend an awful lot of time staring at boxes, don't they?'

Talking to Dad and surfing the Net had got Dido nowhere; she was going to have to find another way of finding the Shadowmaster.

17
Night Calls

Dido and Dad were in the lounge when Mum came home. Mum looked weary, but managed a smile.

'Sorry I'm so late,' she said, 'but I've cleared my desk of paperwork for the first time this term. I think I'm finally getting the hang of this Deputy Head lark.'

Now I wonder why that is? thought Dido, pleased with herself for getting rid of the hex sign, and glad to hear Mum sounding positive.

'Knew you would,' said Dad, 'though I was starting to worry that you were pushing yourself too hard.'

'That's what comes of having a boss like Alan Parker,' Mum said. 'He can be very demanding when he wants to be.'

'Is that *demanding* as in *slave-driver*?' said Dido.

Mum laughed and said, 'No comment.'

Dad stood up and rubbed his hands together.

'How about one of my culinary specials to

celebrate?' he said. 'Any takers for Spag Bol?'

Mum and Dido each raised a hand; Dad went into the kitchen and clattered pans around.

Mum sighed gratefully as she slumped into an armchair.

'Did you go to Philippa's house?' she said.

'Yup.'

'Did she mention anything about—?'

'Nope,' said Dido. 'She's in denial.'

'She's not the only one,' Mum said meaningfully.

'Oh?'

'When I left my office, I saw Alice Morgan on her way home. There wasn't time for me to insee her properly. I just caught a glimpse, but it made me think that you could be right about her.'

'What did you see?'

'Not much,' Mum said. 'It wasn't a seeing as much as a feeling that Alice has power.'

Dido's thumbs twitched.

'Magic?' she said.

'Hard to tell. Alice keeps it buried deep where no one can find it.'

Which is just what a clever Shadowmaster would do if she knew there were Light Witches around, Dido thought. She said, 'Light

Magic or Shadow Magic?'

'What, Alice Morgan – a Shadowmaster?' Mum spluttered. 'I don't think so!'

But Dido wasn't so sure: Mum hadn't been in the Drama studio when Philippa had been bewitched, and she hadn't seen the look on Miss Morgan's face.

'Anyhow, that's enough of Alice Morgan,' Mum said. 'I don't like discussing members of staff with you, Dido. It's unprofessional. I'll insee her again when I get the chance.'

Dido decided on a change of tack, and put out a feeler about one of her leads on the Shadowmaster – the hairs from the silver tabby.

'Mum,' she said, 'you know that spell Light Witches use to locate things people have lost?'

'Y-e-s,' Mum said cautiously.

'Can it be turned around? Like, if I had something and I didn't know who it belonged to, could I find out by reversing the spell?'

'No, and don't even think about trying it. Reversing spells is dangerous.'

'Why?'

'Because that's how—' Mum stopped herself from saying what she'd been about to say. 'Because it is, that's all. You'll just have to take my word for it.'

'Is it something else I'm not ready for yet?'

'Oh, Dido!' Mum said. 'I hate doing this. I know how keen you are to learn, and it must seem as if your father and I are always putting you down because of it, but we do it for a good reason, honestly. We'll explain why one day, I promise.'

Dido thought, One day, some day, some time, never.

Mum's improved mood lasted all evening. She even cracked jokes over dinner, which she hadn't for a while, and the atmosphere in the house relaxed.

Dido made herself scarce and went to bed early, claiming to be tired, which she thought was a fib when she said it, but it turned out to be true. As soon as her head touched the pillow, Dido's eyelids drooped heavily and she yawned.

Breaking that spell on Philippa must've taken more out of me than I realised, she thought.

It was her last thought; a dark pit of sleep opened up beneath her and she dropped right in.

Three things woke Dido: the itching of her thumbs, Cosmo's urgent mewing and a tapping noise. Dido shook her head, blinked sleep away and glanced at the clock radio on her bedside cabinet. It was midnight. She couldn't hear where the tapping was coming from because of Cosmo's din.

'OK, Cosmo,' Dido said. 'I'm awake. Let me listen a second, will you?'

Cosmo wittered something about how young people today showed no respect for their elders, then fell silent.

The tapping came again, a thin, hard sound; the sound of fingernails rattling against glass.

Dido swung herself out of bed and shivered. The bedroom was cold, far colder than it ought to have been. Dido stepped across the room, drew back the curtains – and almost screamed. Fear brought her wide awake, sharpening her eyesight, making everything so clear that it seemed unreal.

Jack Farmer was outside – or something that resembled Jack Farmer. His face was as white as the moon, his eyes were black and empty, and his feet stood on nothing. When he saw Dido, he smiled.

'You have to help me, Dido!' he whispered hoarsely. 'I don't understand what's happening to me, but it hurts. Please help me, Dido, please, please, please!'

Although his voice begged, Jack's smile didn't budge and the contrast was horrible.

'I don't know how I got here!' Jack whined.

'Please do something quickly!'

Dido was torn. Half of her yearned to help Jack, but another, colder half told her not to believe in what she was seeing.

'Who sent you?' she said.

'I don't know!'

Dido thought of what Lilil had told her about asking the right question and said, 'What are you?'

The pleading tone went out of Jack's voice. 'Oh, you're good, Light Witch,' he said admiringly. 'You're very good.'

Dido's Shadow side stepped in to show exactly how good she was, and threw out a spell in the shape of a black hornet. The hornet shot through the window, and the Jack-thing quivered and vanished like a bursting bubble.

Cosmo chattered a question.

'That?' said Dido, pressing her left hand to her thumping heart. 'My guess is that it was the Shadowmaster version of a glamour spell, sort of an optical-illusion thing. See the time? Midnight, the witching hour. How corny can you get?'

But it was worse than corny: the Shadowmaster had treated her like a child.

'That's it!' Dido growled. 'That – is – it! I've had it

up to here with being condescended to.'

Her resentment flared into anger, and with the anger came a revelation. All the moves the Shadowmaster had made against her had been attempts to throw her off the track and frighten her away.

From what? Dido thought. If you're so powerful, why don't you come out in the open and get it over with, Shadowmaster? Why didn't you steal my magic as soon as I arrived? What are you scared of – ME?

And suddenly she knew what she had to do.

'Cosmo?' said Dido. 'I need a favour.'

Cosmo's ears pricked.

'A big favour.'

Cosmo trilled in a what's-in-it-for-me? kind of way.

'Isn't being a faithful familiar reward enough?'

Cosmo meowed the Cat for, 'Get outta here!'

'Tell you what,' said Dido, 'I'll get a pack of those cheesy treats Mum won't buy you and slip them to you on the quiet. In return, I want you to show me where Mum and Dad have stashed the magic book they won't let me look at.'

Cosmo yowled unhappily.

'Yes, I know what they'd do to us if they found out, but I won't tell if you won't,' said Dido. 'And besides, if I don't get my act together ASAP, something awful's going to happen to them and me, and if we're not around, who'll feed *you*?'

That clinched it for Cosmo. She hopped off the bed, headed out of the door on to the landing, launched herself at the door of Dad's study and opened it by flipping the door handle with her front paws. Dido took the silver tabby's hairs from the drawer of her cabinet and followed Cosmo into the room. Cosmo vaulted on to Dad's desk and turned on the desk light.

The study was lined with shelves that held row on row of technical manuals. The titles on the spines were so boring that Dido couldn't imagine anybody wanting to read one. It was the perfect place to hide a book of magic, and so obvious that Dido would never have thought of looking there unless Cosmo had led her to it.

Cosmo walked across the desk, raised her tail and swept its tip across the spine of *Advanced Networking For Beginners*. Dido went into inseeing and saw that the book was surrounded by a protective spell. The spell was so Dad that Dido grinned at it. It must have been taken from a childhood memory of his – a wooden shed on an allotment. The planks of the shed were warped and green with age. The door was held shut by a massive old-fashioned padlock.

Knowing Dad, the spell was nowhere near as ramshackle as it looked, and Dido approached it gingerly. She reached deep inside her Light Magic and thought of the right key – short, stubby, its pitted steel barrel shiny from use. She placed it in the keyhole, turned, and the padlock sprang open with a satisfyingly loud snick.

The shed disappeared; Dido stretched out her hand and took something down from the shelf.

The book was battered, with dusty, wrinkled pages covered in crabbed handwriting that was hard to decipher until Dido got used to it.

The title page read,

A Grimoire of Sundrie Spelles of the Arte of Magick

The spelling was the same all the way through, archaic enough to give an English teacher a fit, but Dido had studied enough old books to have no problem in understanding it, and before long she found what she wanted.

To Discover an Enemy
Lay hands on something belonging to thy rival and
hold it close in thy left hand. When thou hast wound
thyself in charms and talismans, speak thus:
All-seeing Lady of the Light,
Show me mine enemy this night.
Be it man, or maiden fair,
Or spirit riding through the air,
Let their visage now appear.

That straightforward, huh? Dido thought. The cat hairs would do for something belonging to the Shadowmaster; as for charms and talismans, she would have to depend on her magic skills.

Dido sat down on Dad's swivel chair, with the grimoire open in front of her. Cosmo stepped off the desk on to her lap.

'Hey, what's this?' Dido protested.

Cosmo told her.

'But I don't need you to assist me,' said Dido.

Cosmo disagreed, and sunk her claws into Dido's thighs.

'Ouch! All right, have it your way.'

Dido concentrated and whispered the verse aloud.

The cat hairs glowed brightly. The light from them spread across the opened book and the words on the pages began to move, wiggling like maggots. They dropped on to the desk and crawled towards Dido.

Cosmo hissed out a warning. Dido tried to call back the discovery spell, but it pulled her and Cosmo along with it. A spidery tickling on Dido's skin marked the progress of the words as they crept up her arm, along her shoulder and on to her face, filling her eyes with darkness.

18
Beyond the Ghost Fence

Dido panicked, kicking, and flailing her arms. She tried to yell the Goddess's name, but she had no voice. Fear grabbed her like an iron band squeezing her around the chest.

Then she saw Cosmo. Cosmo didn't look in the least frightened. She was padding along with her tail held high. The fact that there wasn't anything for her paws to step on didn't seem to bother her.

Dido caught some of Cosmo's calm and the iron band slackened enough for her to take in her surroundings. She didn't seem to have fallen into a trap, as she'd feared. The discovery spell was working in a totally unexpected way. Dido had figured that she'd have a vision of a face, or hear a voice, but the spell was carrying her and Cosmo somewhere, and the ride was First Class. It felt nothing like the booby-trapped spell that had caught her at The Pentacle. It was smoother, gentler, reminding Dido of the moving walkway she'd once used at Heathrow Airport, or a ride in a lift – except that she didn't seem to be moving forwards, backwards, up or down. The darkness all around her was pleasantly warm, and satiny-smooth on her fingertips. This was a different kind of magic, neither Light nor Shadow, and Dido's intuition told her that it was older than both.

Maybe if I relax and stay cool, things will be OK, she thought.

The darkness began to ripple and solidify, and everything changed.

The spell left Dido and Cosmo on a path in a forest that was bathed in moonlight. In front of them was a marble fountain, half black, half white. Jets of water came from the mouths of two carved faces and splashed into a round basin. The white face was the face of the Goddess, serene and kind, wise-eyed; she wore the horns of the new moon on her head, and the water that played from her mouth gleamed silver.

The dark head was male. It too wore a crescent crown, but there its resemblance to the Goddess ended. It had a hard face, with a hooked nose and heavy-lidded eyes; its wide mouth was spread into a mocking leer.

Dido was puzzled.

'Who is that, Cosmo?' she whispered.

Cosmo mewed impatiently.

Dido didn't know whether it was the effect of the spell or the place itself, but the understanding between her and Cosmo had gone on to a higher level, and she knew exactly what Cosmo was thinking.

'Well I don't know which way to go, do I?' said Dido. 'I've not been here before. You're the one who's supposed to be the guide.'

Cosmo turned her head to the right and sniffed, then turned to the left. She set off down the path, following the gaze of the black marble eyes.

The left-hand path, thought Dido. The dark way – yeah, that'd be right.

She followed Cosmo into the forest.

The path was dappled with moonlight and shadow, and sloped upwards. An owl swooped silently over Dido's head, sending her pulse rocketing.

Cosmo warbled.

'Sure, I'll bet there are plenty of mice, but don't go hunting them now,' Dido said. 'Leave them alone and—'

From far off came the lonely howling of a wolf.

Dido shivered, and hoped that leaving things alone worked both ways.

As she climbed higher, Dido's thumbs started to itch – a hot itching, as if she'd been packing snowballs with her bare hands. It wasn't long before the source of the itching became apparent.

The path levelled out and came to an abrupt halt at the foot of a fence. The fence had been built with thick wooden stakes, three metres high, and the top of each stake had been whittled to a sharp point. Round objects were fixed to the points, and when Dido drew closer she saw to her horror that they were human heads. Some looked fresh and their stakes were streaked with blood; others were older, with empty eye sockets; a few were skulls, dry and weathered.

Dido had read about such fences – ghost fences, erected to ward off hostile spirits – or Light Witches – but nothing she'd read had prepared her for the horror of the real thing, or the sickening smell of rotting flesh. Dido had always considered that evil had an intelligence behind it, but there was nothing intelligent about the ghost fence. It was cruel, mindless and filthy. Her stomach churned.

'I think I may have to throw up,' she warned Cosmo.

Cosmo told her that there was work to be done, and to get a grip.

Dido cast an unlocking spell that had revolving doors, popping coffee-jar seals and ripping envelopes in it, and when that failed, the strongest forcing spell she knew – a mix of tanks and battering-rams. The ghost fence brushed it off as if it were no more than an annoying bluebottle.

'Any suggestions, Cosmo?' Dido said.

Cosmo's suggestion was short and pithy, and translated into Human as, 'Zap the sucker!'

'I'm trying, I'm trying!' said Dido.

Dive-bombers failed to demolish the fence; a herd of stampeding elephants passed straight through and left it unscathed. Dido attempted to make a door or an archway appear, but the fence stubbornly resisted her.

She took a break and called up all she knew about ghost fences. They were intended to inspire fear, to make anybody who encountered one believe that the worst death they could imagine lay waiting on the other side. That made Dido think of other things that were designed to frighten people – such as bungee-jumping, and Halloween outfits.

A spell stirred in her Shadow Magic. The spell was massive, shaped like a storm cloud. The cloud hung over the ghost fence and hurled down lashing sheets of rain. The rain only lasted a few seconds, and ended with a peal of thunder, but when the storm was over, the fence had been transformed.

It looked pathetic, like part of a fairground's haunted house. The stakes were crudely painted in lurid colours on to a sheet of hardboard. The heads were papier-maché, pulpy from the downpour that had drenched them.

'Way to go, Dido!' Cosmo said in Cat.

Dido stepped up to the ghost fence, pushed it and the entire structure collapsed.

'Could do better, Shadowmaster,' Dido said.

She and Cosmo walked over the remains of the fence. The trees thinned and they came out into the open.

Dido wasn't surprised to see the Speaking Stones straight ahead of her, or the fire blazing within the circle, or the figure standing in front of the fire.

She heard the same chanting as before:

'*Palecorum alnech la,*
Saletarum detha na,
Vida nectus,
Kalam si,
Talla mectus ifte da.'

Closer to, Dido could make out the figure more clearly – a man, dressed in animals' skins. His arms were bare and there was a pentagram tattooed on his left bicep. His face was hidden behind a stag's head mask with a sweeping spread of antlers. The silver tabby was seated on the ground beside him. The cat spat at Cosmo, and Cosmo spat back.

'*Valle tilere, Lilil,*' the man said.

Dido was astonished that he knew her secret magic name, but didn't let the astonishment show as she said, 'I don't speak your language, Shadowmaster, and I'm Dido, not Lilil.'

'I know who you are,' the Shadowmaster said. His voice was deep and naggingly familiar, but disguised by magic. 'My lord and I have long awaited this moment. We have hunted you through lifetime after lifetime, and now we have found you again at last.'

'Your lord?' said Dido. 'Let's see now, that would be Spelkor, wouldn't it?'

'I do not take his name lightly in this place, child.'

Dido rankled at *child*, but kept her temper, guessing that the Shadowmaster was hoping to goad her into losing control.

'Where are we?' she said.

'At the Speaking Stones.'

Wrong question, thought Dido, and said, '*When* are we?'

'In Shadow Magic there are places outside time.'

'And we're here because?'

The Shadowmaster laughed.

'The years have not dulled your wits, Lilil, but as yet this child has a poor grasp of your memories,' he said. 'She is too young to know that we were once partners – the greatest witches of our age. None dared to stand against us. We were glorious.'

Partners? thought Dido. Then she remembered what Lilil had told her about being reborn. Like Lilil, the Shadowmaster's witch-spirit must have been reincarnated many times, and in one of those lives he and Lilil had made magic together.

Dido couldn't afford herself the luxury of working her way through all this, and set it aside. 'Guess that was back in the good old days, huh?' she said.

'Don't mock me, Light Witch!' the Shadowmaster said harshly. 'I could destroy you in the blinking of an eye.'

'If you were going to destroy me, you would have done it ages ago. So why didn't you?'

'Because I follow a higher purpose,' said the

Shadowmaster. 'A purpose that was first written in fire on the topmost peaks of...'

Dido switched off.

He's enjoying this, she thought. Boy, he just loves the sound of his own voice. He's like a boring teacher, droning on and on.

The Shadowmaster was in full flow now. '...my lord, the master of despair and sorrow, the master of tricks and lies, the master of darkness and dismay...'

And Dido knew who he was, magic voice or not. She waited for him to take a breath and said, 'That mask must be uncomfortable. Why don't you take it off, Mr Purdey?'

Mr Purdey raised his hands to his head, removed the mask and let it drop on to the grass. 'It took you longer to find me out than I expected,' he said in his normal voice.

Dido remembered that the hex sign on Mum's office door had revealed the Shadowmaster's vanity and decided to use it against him.

'You led me quite a dance,' she said. 'I thought you were Miss Morgan.'

Mr Purdey was flattered, and smiled.

'How gratifying,' he said. 'I enjoy deceit, and I

thrive on misery. Happiness comes and goes in a laugh, but pain and suffering endure far longer. Over the years, Prince Arthur's has been a rich source of both emotions. Few pleasures can match the unhappiness of young minds.'

'You're clever,' said Dido. 'I would never have suspected you. Is it your curse that's messing up Stanstowe? That must've taken some doing.'

'A curse like that is beyond my ability, and Stanstowe isn't cursed, it's privileged.'

Dido couldn't make head or tail of this.

'Let's get to the point,' she said. 'Tell me about the higher purpose again, but leave out the stuff about the fiery writing and the peaks of wherever.'

'You deserted me, Lilil,' said Mr Purdey. 'You turned aside from the darkness and refused its delights, but it's not too late. Come back to me. Let us unite and be as we were, wealthy and mighty. Join your force with mine, and the world we live in will bow down before us.'

Dido was confused. Who was talking – Mr Purdey, the Stanstowe Shadowmaster, his witch-spirit, or was the mysterious lord he'd spoken of using him as a microphone? It was impossible to tell.

'And if I say no?' Dido asked.

'I will lay waste your mind and your magic, and you will be nothing.'

Dido felt a stab of fear, but was determined not to give in. She shook her head.

'No deal,' she said. 'If I join with you, you'll do even more damage. I'll become like you, and I'd rather be nothing than a monster.'

Mr Purdey's eyes widened.

'Then you're trapped inside the body of a fool, Lilil!' he said. He lifted his face upwards and shouted, 'I call upon you, Spelkor, Lord of the Night. Lend me a little of your strength so I may work your will!'

As his voice rang out, Cosmo streaked across the circle and pounced on the silver tabby. They rolled together, growling and squealing, ripping tufts of dark and silver fur from each others' coats.

Overhead, hundreds of shooting stars zipped across the sky. They massed into a pulsing purple ball that hurtled straight at Dido. The spell had no form; it was raw power.

Dido heard her Shadow Magic sing for joy. It roared inside her and through her, sending out a blue aura that surrounded her. The aura absorbed the impact of the purple ball and shattered it, scattering sparks in all directions.

Dido was exhilarated; her magic was far greater in the timeless place, and worked without her having to shape it.

Mr Purdey cursed and extended his left arm. A bolt of purple lightning crackled out of the centre of his palm.

Dido's hand mirrored the movement; the lightning that sprang from her palm was blue. The two bolts locked together and writhed around each other, twirling into a spiral.

Sweat trickled down Mr Purdey's face, orange in the glow of the fire.

'You cannot resist me, child!' he muttered through gritted teeth. 'I am older and more skilled than you. You will surrender to me. My magic must prevail!'

But Dido's magic was relentless. Its blueness followed the purple bolt, creeping closer and closer to Mr Purdey, sucking the power from his spell and turning it back on him. Mr Purdey's knees buckled. He sank down on the ground, sobbing; his lightning sputtered and died.

'Help me, Lord Spelkor!' he cried out.

The circle moved. The surface of the stones flowed like melting plastic. Heads and limbs grew out of them and they turned into huge dog-like animals of flesh and stone, with slavering jaws and burning red eyes. They loped towards Mr Purdey, the lope speeding into a charge, then into a grey blur that Dido's eyes couldn't penetrate. The blur circled Mr Purdey.

A strangled moan of desperation was swallowed into silence; then the stones resumed their places and their shapes.

Cosmo found that she was fighting emptiness; the silver tabby had disappeared, and she hissed in frustrated anger.

Dido lurched forward. She felt used-up, as empty as Christmas wrapping paper on Boxing Day, and far too exhausted to be triumphant.

'You've done well, Dido,' said a voice.

Dido turned; Lilil was standing behind her.

'Is the Shadowmaster—?' said Dido.

'Spelkor does not tolerate failure. The Shadowmaster's body still lives, but his magic is dead. He won't threaten you again.'

'But I thought it was only the Goddess who could—?'

'Light Witches follow the Goddess,' said Lilil. 'Shadowmasters walk in the ways of Spelkor.'

Dido's weariness made this difficult to follow.

'What'll happen to Mr Purdey in my world?'

'He'll fall ill,' said Lilil. 'When he recovers, he won't remember anything about Shadow Magic. He'll be an ordinary man.'

'Won't he be punished for what he did?'

Lilil smiled sadly and said, 'If the spirit that makes you a witch was taken away from you, wouldn't you count that as a punishment? You must go home and rest now, Dido. This battle is over, but other battles lie ahead. The Speaking Stones aren't finished with you yet.'

'The Speaking Stones,' Dido said thoughtfully. 'Were they originally called the Spelkor Stones by any chance?'

'Rest,' Lilil insisted.

The circle was fading fast. Dido could see the outline of Dad's desk lamp through the stones.

'Hang on!' said Dido. 'I've got about a million questions I want to ask.'

But she was already back in Dad's study, and she had a faceful of cat. Cosmo was standing on her lap, front paws pressed against her shoulders, rubbing her head against Dido's face and purring deeply.

Dido scratched Cosmo behind the ears and said, 'We made it, Coz! Let's hope we don't have to do that again in a hurry.'

Cosmo jumped on to the floor and miaowed.

'Too right I'm knackered,' Dido said. 'You go on into my bedroom, I'll be there in a minute. I have to put this grimoire back and replace the protection spell on it.'

She barely had the strength left to do either. Dido felt that she could sleep for at least a week.

19

The Portrait

Mum's mobile rang while the Nesbits were having breakfast next morning. Mum went to the kitchen to take the call, and when she came back into the dining room, her face was serious.

'I've got some bad news, I'm afraid,' she said to Dido.

'Oh?' said Dido, knowing already what the bad news would be.

'Hugh Purdey has been taken to hospital with a suspected minor stroke.'

'Is it serious – will he be all right?'

'It's too soon to tell. I'll ring the hospital later and find out how he is.' Mum consulted her watch. 'I'd better go into school early and sort out cover for his lessons.'

After Mum had left, Dad said, 'Hugh Purdey? He's your form tutor, isn't he?'

'Yes,' said Dido.

She was confused. Mr Purdey's illness affected her more than she'd expected; she felt responsible and guilty. Even though she'd had no choice about defending herself against Mr Purdey the Shadowmaster, the result had damaged Mr Purdey the man, and harming other people went against everything Dido had been taught about magic. Worst of all, when her Shadow side had taken over, she'd revelled in it; for a split second she'd had a taste of what it was like to be a Shadowmaster, and the taste had been exciting. Dido realised that she had a lot to learn about her magic, and herself.

'Dad,' she said, 'if you had to do something that you knew was wrong, to help you do something that you knew was right, would you?'

Dad grimaced.

'Give me a break, Dido!' he groaned. 'It's eight o' clock in the morning, and that's a major philosophical question.'

'But would you?'

Dad took a gulp of coffee for inspiration.

'That would depend on how wrong the wrong thing was, and how right the right thing was.'

'And if you made a mistake?'

'I'd learn from it and move on,' said Dad. 'It's

called growing up.' He peered closely at Dido. 'Are you feeling all right this morning? You look a little green around the gills.'

Dido had prepared herself for a question along these lines.

'Rough night,' she said. 'Cosmo woke me up and it took me ages to get back to sleep.'

'You're too soft with that cat. I should fit a lock to your door so you can shut her out of your bedroom at night.'

'We tried that once in the old house, remember? She ripped up the landing carpet and we had to buy another. It's cheaper to let her sleep on my bed. Anyway, Cosmo isn't any old cat, she's my familiar.'

'Considering what she gets up to, don't you mean that she's your *strange*?'

It was Dido's turn to wince.

'Dad, it's eight o' clock in the morning,' she said. 'It's too early for bad jokes, OK?'

In the bus on the way to school, Scott turned to Dido and said, 'Cop this!'

He held a piece of string between the thumb and index finger of his left hand. In the middle of the string was a tight knot. Scott waved his right hand over the string, and the knot disappeared.

'Hey, I'm impressed!' said Dido, laughing. 'How's it done?'

'Magic,' said Scott. 'My kind of magic, that is, not yours. Know what's weird?'

'What?'

'I've been trying to crack that trick for months, but I couldn't get the hang of it. Then this morning I gave it a go and I could do it, just like that. Funny, isn't it?'

Dido didn't think that it was funny. Her guess was that now Mr Purdey's influence had been removed, a lot of Prince Arthur's pupils would find things were going right for them at last.

Scott lowered his voice.

'Any luck with finding the you-know-who?'

'Done and dusted,' Dido said.

'Really – who was it?'

'That's private.'

'Aw, go on! You can tell me.'

'OK, you know the guy who presents that gardening programme on Friday nights? It was him.'

Scott gasped, then screwed up his mouth.

'You're having me on, aren't you?' he said.

'Corr-ect!'

'You're not going to tell me who it is, are you?'

'Congratulations, Scott Pink!' said Dido. 'You've won tonight's star prize, a day in the Prince Arthur Comprehensive School, Stanstowe.'

Dido had been right about the changes at school. After Scott had passed through the main gate, he suddenly stopped dead and looked around suspiciously.

'What's different?' he said.

'Nothing,' said Dido.

'No, something's different. School looks brighter. Has it been redecorated or something?'

Dido used her inseeing. Prince Arthur's was as busy and chaotic as ever, but the edginess had gone from the atmosphere; the school felt happier, more relaxed.

'Must be the sunshine,' said Dido. 'It tends to brighten things up.'

Philippa had brightened up too. As Scott and Dido were walking towards C Block, Philippa came bouncing over to them, all smiles, and said, 'Guess what? You'll never guess!'

'You'd better tell us then,' said Dido.

'Mr Purdey's off sick, and we're going to have Miss Morgan as our form tutor!'

'The mystery woman,' said Dido, thinking aloud.

'Huh?' Scott said. 'Why is Miss Morgan the mystery woman?'

'Did I say mystery?' said Dido, backtracking frantically. 'I meant dramatic. Miss Morgan's very dramatic, isn't she?'

'Er, hello?' said Scott. 'She's a Drama teacher.'

As it turned out there was nothing dramatic or mysterious about registration – it was simply routine. While Miss Morgan called the register, Dido took the opportunity to check out Jack Farmer. He was clean; the mischief spell had been lifted from him. He was still a troublemaker, but he wasn't a bewitched troublemaker any more.

Dido resisted the temptation to insee Miss Morgan. She'd had enough magic and teachers to last for a long while.

Wandering around the campus at lunchtime, Dido, Scott and Philippa met up with Ollie. Scott insisted on demonstrating his knot trick, and Philippa was so tickled by it, she asked him to show her again.

Ollie caught Dido's eye, and they drifted a few steps away.

'What did you do?' Ollie said.

'About what?'

'The curse.'

'Oh, a bit of magic,' Dido said casually. 'A bat's wing here, a newt's eye there, that kind of thing. Has the curse gone?'

She was hoping to hear that it had, but instead Ollie said, 'No, but it's weaker, like it's gone into hibernation.'

Lilil's voice came back to Dido. '…Other battles lie ahead. The Speaking Stones aren't finished with you yet.'

'Let's keep our fingers crossed that it stays asleep,' said Dido.

The bombshell dropped a few days later. Mum sent a message to Dido during last lesson, telling her to report to her office after school. Dido thought that something might have happened to Dad or Cosmo, and when the final bell went she hurried through the corridors. But when she got into the office, Dido saw that she had nothing to worry about. Mum looked unconcerned, and was holding a large bouquet of flowers wrapped in shiny pink paper.

'Who are the flowers for?' said Dido.

'Hugh Purdey,' Mum said. 'I'm about to go and visit him at the hospital. Want to come along?'

'Er...actually, I might give it a miss.'

'He's asked to see you.'

Dido felt as though the ceiling had dropped on her head.

'Me?' she yelped. 'What for?'

'Maybe he's fond of you. Teachers do have feelings you know, despite what pupils think.'

Dido tried to wriggle her way out.

'I've got tonnes of homework,' she said. 'And I wouldn't want to tire Mr Purdey out or anything.'

'If he's asked to see you, he must feel up to it,' Mum said reasonably. 'He could probably do with a friendly face to cheer him up. It must be incredibly boring to be stuck in bed all day.'

Mum's tone was quietly insistent; Dido knew there was no way out, and gave in with as much grace as she could muster. Her thumbs weren't giving her any warning signs, but she had butterflies in her stomach the size of ostriches. She wasn't looking forward to meeting the first victim of her witchcraft.

*

Mr Purdey was in a men's ward; his bed was close to the double doors. There was only one get-well card on his bedside cupboard – probably from Mum or Dr Parker, Dido thought.

Mr Purdey looked worn out. His hair had turned grey and there were deep lines at the sides of his mouth. When he saw Mum and Dido, he smiled.

'I've brought you some flowers, Hugh,' Mum said, waving the bouquet. 'I'll ask one of the nurses for a vase. Shan't be long.'

She bustled off into the corridor.

Dido sat down in the chair beside Mr Purdey's bed. There was an awkward silence, then Dido forced herself to say, 'How are you feeling, Mr Purdey?'

'A bit better, thank you, Dido,' Mr Purdey said slowly. 'Talking was difficult at first, but the speech therapist tells me I'm making great strides. It was good of you to come.'

'Seven North miss you. Miss Morgan takes the register now. She's OK, but everybody wonders when you're coming back,' Dido gabbled nervously.

'It's kind of you to lie, Dido, but I'm quite sure that most of my pupils are pleased by my absence. I've never been a popular member of staff. As to coming back, I doubt that I will. Having a stroke –

even a mild one, like mine – puts a new perspective on life. Like everyone, I once dreamed of having wealth and fame, but the dreams proved hollow. I have a suspicion that I won't get as much out of teaching as I used to. Something appears to be missing.'

Dido looked straight into Mr Purdey's eyes, and saw a vulnerability in them. She wondered what kind of person he'd been before Shadow Magic had taken him over, and when and how it had happened, but she'd never know. Mr Purdey's memory had been wiped clean by the entity he'd served.

'D'you remember anything, Mr Purdey?' Dido asked softly.

'Remember?'

'About what happened the night you were taken ill.'

A distant expression came into Mr Purdey's eyes.

'I remember waking in the night and feeling odd,' he said, 'and the next thing I remember is being here in hospital. I did have a peculiar dream, though. It was about you.'

'Was it?' said Dido.

'It was complete nonsense, of course. You know how incoherent dreams can be.'

'Why did you ask to see me?'

Mr Purdey was troubled by the question.

'I don't know why, but I felt as if I owed you an apology,' he said. 'Perhaps I did or said something that...' He frowned and shook his head. 'No, it's gone.'

'I'm sorry too, Mr Purdey.'

'What for?'

'That you're ill.'

'There's no need for you to feel sorry, Dido,' said Mr Purdey. 'It isn't as if my illness is your fault, is it? We bring these things on ourselves.'

And Dido felt, in some strange way, that Mr Purdey was forgiving her.

During the car ride home, Mum said, 'Oh, by the way, I insaw Alice Morgan this morning.'

'And?' said Dido.

'She's a Sleeper.'

'A what?'

'A Sleeper,' Mum said again. 'Sleepers have magical powers, but they're not aware of having them. Alice uses her magic to teach, without realising that she's doing it. She's unable to cast spells, of course, but magic can help her in other ways.'

'Such as charming the socks off her classes?'

'Yes, but it does no harm.'

'Are you going to tell her that she's a Sleeper?'

'I'm not sure that I ought to,' said Mum. 'Sleepers are like sleepwalkers, it can be dangerous to wake them.'

'Are Sleepers rare?'

'No,' Mum said. 'Most people have got some magic inside them. Some have more magic than others.'

'And some,' Dido thought, 'have got more magic than anyone else realises.'

The following Saturday afternoon, Dido went into town to meet Philippa and Ollie, caught an earlier bus than she usually did, and arrived with time to kill. Not being the sort of person who could wait patiently next to a statue of Queen Victoria for half an hour, Dido decided to investigate the Stanstowe Museum, which formed part of the Town Hall.

The museum had been founded by the Victorians, and it showed. Downstairs was mostly stuffed animals – creepy and sad – and a collection of nineteenth-century biscuit tins, which Dido thought would be fascinating for anyone who was interested in nineteenth-century biscuits.

But when she went upstairs, Dido received a shock, because an engraved brass plate fixed above a doorway said, The Langley-Davis Memorial Wing.

Then Dido entered a room that seemed to be entirely devoted to the Speaking Stones. There was an artist's reconstruction of how the circle might have been built, cases of flint scrapers, hand-axes, and broken pieces of deer-antler picks. In the centre of the room was a model of the circle in a display cabinet with a glass lid. Dido took it all in with a glance – and then her attention was grabbed by something on the wall at the far end of the room – a full-length portrait of a man.

She knew who it would be, even before she read the inscription on the bottom of the frame.

EDWIN LANGLEY-DAVIS,
THE FIRST LORD STANSTOWE (1844-1921)

The portrait had been painted when Edwin was in his fifties, Dido guessed. Unlike many successful men of his time he was slim, but wore a typically Victorian outfit: a pin-striped charcoal grey suit with a watch-chain looped across the waistcoat, a maroon silk cravat, and a shirt with a winged collar that looked way too tight.

Edwin had an unremarkable face, fleshy-nosed and pale-eyed. He seemed sad, but that might have had something to do with the drooping corners of his luxuriant moustache. The most remarkable thing about him was that he was standing outdoors.

Dido recognised the location at once. Behind Edwin's left shoulder was Stanstowe Hill and the Speaking Stones, lit by a single ray of sunlight shining through a sky covered with dark clouds.

Dido's thumbs itched. As she scratched them, a purple aura stood out around the frame of the portrait, and the painted clouds began to glide across the sky. The trees' branches swayed.

Edwin opened his mouth and said, 'Spelkor is waiting, Light Witch. You have the upper hand just now, but be warned that it will not always be so. You have defeated the latest Shadowmaster, and I salute you. Savour your victory while you may, for Spelkor will have revenge in the end. He is sleeping, but he will awaken when the time of the stars is right, and that day will dawn sooner than you might suppose.'

Dido was afraid, but thought that if she could stand up to the ghost fence and Mr Purdey, she could stand up to anything.

'Who are you?' she whispered.

'A man who died long ago, a man who can do you no harm. A visitor from a bygone age.'

'And the Stanstowe Shadowmaster of your day?' Dido wondered aloud.

But the portrait was still again; she was talking to paint on canvas.

Hardly aware of where she was going, Dido stumbled out of the room, down the stairs and into the street. She stood on the pavement, taking deep breaths of air that smelled of exhaust fumes.

The full weight of what Lilil had told her about future battles sank in.

It isn't over! she thought. It isn't over. I have to go through it all again. How many people will I have to hurt? How many people are going to get hurt because of me? And why *me*?

For a moment Dido teetered on the edge of despair. Darkness gathered around her, wailing voices drifted in the wind, panther eyes gleamed in the shadowy doorway across the street. All the buildings surrounding her wavered like reflections on a lake.

Something older was rising from the depths. It would break the surface any second...

Dido closed her ears and eyes and forced herself back into the light.

Listen, Dido!' she thought. You have two choices. You can either stress about this magic stuff until you crack up, or you can hang out with Philippa and Ollie, have a few laughs and get on with your life. Which is it going to be?

There was no contest: Dido opened her eyes, turned to her left and headed back towards the statue of Queen Victoria to wait for her friends.

More Orchard Red Apples

The Fire Within	Chris d'Lacey	1 84121 533 3
The Salt Pirates of Skegness	Chris d'Lacey	1 84121 539 2
The Poltergoose	Michael Lawrence	1 86039 836 7
The Killer Underpants	Michael Lawrence	1 84121 713 1
The Toilet of Doom	Michael Lawrence	1 84121 752 2
Maggot Pie	Michael Lawrence	1 84121 756 5
Do Not Read This Book	Pat Moon	1 84121 435 3
Do Not Read Any Further	Pat Moon	1 84121 456 6
How to Eat Fried Worms	Thomas Rockwell	1 84362 206 8
How to Get Fabulously Rich	Thomas Rockwell	1 84362 207 6
How to Fight a Girl	Thomas Rockwell	1 84362 208 4

All books priced at £4.99

Orchard Red Apples are available from all good bookshops,
or can be ordered direct from the publisher: Orchard Books,
PO BOX 29, Douglas IM99 1BQ
Credit card orders please telephone 01624 836000
or fax 01624 837033 or visit our Internet site: www.wattspub.co.uk
or e-mail: bookshop@enterprise.net for details.

To order please quote title, author and ISBN
and your full name and address.
Cheques and postal orders should be made payable to 'Bookpost plc.'
Postage and packing is FREE within the UK
(overseas customers should add £1.00 per book).

Prices and availability are subject to change.